Ross and O'Neill Adventures

Galileo's Pendulum

GALILEO'S PENDULUM

A ROSS AND O'NEILL ADVENTURE

KAT SIMONS

GALILEO'S PENDULUM

To my three heroes—my husband and sons.

And to the other lovers of older action-adventure movie…

ONE

JACQUE CAME out of the small galley kitchen in his flat along the Rhine, cup of steaming oolong tea in hand. Satisfied with his week's work and ready for his nightly ritual. A well-earned ritual, if he did say so himself.

The Venetian glass standing mirror had been delivered, the money deposited in Jacque's account in Switzerland just that day. The difficulty with acquiring the seventeenth century German armoire had been settled only an hour ago, which would please the American so desperate to reclaim his German roots. And Jacque had heard nothing from his most…exacting client in the week since the artifact the man had requested had been delivered. Which meant he suspected nothing.

Which meant Jacque had earned tonight's tea.

His study danced with pink-orange shadows in the light from the flickering wood fire in his brick fireplace. The carved wooden mantal over it an elegant piece inherited from his grandfather. The mantal turned what had been a rather ordinary fireplace into a show piece, as was more appropriate for Jacque's study. He considered one of the Tiffany lamps in the corner, but discarded the idea of adding more than firelight to the room.

Hollowell preferred their tea time to be quiet and dark. So did Jacque.

"Pss pss," he called. "Hollowell. It's time for our tea."

An oversized orange tabby cat sauntered through the bedroom doorway, his tail twitching as he crossed the inlaid hardwood floor. Heated tiles for the floors in the sitting room, the kitchen, his main office, and the entryway. But in here, Jacque loved the texture of the hardwood underfoot. The slight creak and bounce. He hadn't even bothered with rugs. He'd had the floors installed not long after moving into the flat, when he'd had the hand-carved wooden bookshelves that lined the walls placed. Thirty years ago now. Such a long time to be in the same location for a man like him. But he was careful. Always very careful. He only worked with the best. That helped. The profits he made bought a lot of leverage as well.

And it wasn't as if he could hide from his clients. Not the specific and very wealthy ones he catered to. They'd find him, no matter where he lived. Better to be in a comfortable home, secured by an alarm system and a small contingent of guards on the first floor. Nothing extravagant. He preferred to put his money into his own antiques collection—he didn't sell everything, and he wanted to retire one day. But a handful of men who could warn him if anything was amiss.

He settled into his favorite antique, Queen Anne wingback, freshly reupholstered just two weeks ago. The smell of oolong and woodsmoke had finally started to overpower the smell of fresh velvet and upholstery glue. Velvet had been, perhaps, a risky choice with Hollowell. But Jacque's house cleaner loved the cat enough to only charge Jacque a little more for cleaning cat hair out of velvet regularly.

He cupped the warm ceramic mug in his hands, the warmth seeping in. His hands got colder these days. Age, and his preference for living beside the river in Vienna didn't help. His thick Irish wool sweater and flannel trousers kept most of his aging body comfortable on these damp early spring nights, but nothing short of gloves, or a very hot cup of tea, kept his hands warm. As he breathed in deeply of oolong, he realized Hollowell hadn't jumped into his lap yet. He glanced across to see the tom paused halfway through the room, his large body rigid, the hair along his back and tail puffed.

"Oh," Jacque said, making a face at the cat. "Are you mad at me that we're late? Come come. I was not so long. And the schrank has been secured for the obnoxious American. We must celebrate. We'll sit and drink our tea, and I'll give you enough attention to make up for being distracted during dinner."

Hollowell hissed, suddenly, viciously. Then spun and raced away faster than Jacque had ever seen the big cat move.

He half rose from his seat. "Hollowell?"

A rough hand pushed him back into the chair.

Jacque's heartbeat accelerated instantly. He gripped his mug tighter as panic rushed through his limbs. Who? How? He hadn't forgotten to set the alarm. The men downstairs…had they missed something?

Jacque looked around, frantic, his hands beginning to shake, spilling hot tea into is lap. He barely noticed the burn as the liquid seeped through his flannel pants. Two men stood beside his chair, large men in dark suits, both staring straight ahead. Where had they come from? How had he missed them? The study was very dark. No light leaked in through the closed velvet curtains which normally provided an excellent view of the Rhine. The darkness left the corners in shadows. But shadows deep enough to hid such large men?

"You sold me a fake, Jacque." A voice from the far shadows, hidden in the darkness behind the nineteenth century French library table Jacque used for a desk sometimes. A voice thick was a heavy Russian accent.

Panic clenched around Jacque's throat now. He couldn't swallow. No. This wasn't possible. The Russian couldn't have known. He couldn't be here. Jacque's men. Why hadn't they warned him?

The thought that his men downstairs might be dead flittered through Jacque's mind. And more panic surged. Dead or paid off. The man hiding in the dark corner of the room could do either. Whatever he felt most expedient. Jacque knew working with the Russian was dangerous when he'd taken the man's request. But he'd been so certain, so sure…

A vague silhouette stepped away from the deeper shadows, coming just far enough forward Jacque could make out his large, broad-shouldered frame.

"I…" Jacque stuttered. "No. I wouldn't."

The words had barely left his mouth when the man came far enough forward for Jacque to see his face in the orange firelight.

He gasped and pressed back into his seat, even though he'd known what to expect. Anton Mikhailov was as large as the men who served him, though many years older. Unlike Jacque, the years hadn't hunched the Russian's broad shoulders, though, and the gray in his blond hair turned his shortly buzzed style a distinguished silver. His pale white skin combined with that silver hair gave the Russian a very icy look. Cold. Like his dark eyes. As cold and dark as the Rhine at night in midwinter.

"I did nothing," Jacque said, his voice barely a whisper around the fear clogging his throat. "I would never sell you anything that wasn't authentic. I swear."

"Who made the forgery?" the Russian said, his voice quiet and hard as steel.

"It's not…"

The large man to the right of Jacque pulled a gun from beneath his suit jacket. The man on the left slipped a huge hunting knife from beneath his tailored coat.

Jacque swallowed, or tried to. His grip on his mug slipped. The ceramic crashed to the floor, tea spilling across the hardwood. "They swore it was authentic," he rasped. "It is not my fault."

"Who?" the Russian said.

Jacque hesitated. A moment. Not long. But long enough to regret what he was about to do. Only a little, though. If she'd done her job. If she'd done a *good* job, the Russian wouldn't be here, in Jacque's home, staring at him with those icy dark eyes as his men held a gun and a knife beside Jacque's head. Jacque only worked with the best. She was supposed to be the best. And yet, the Russian was here. In Jacque's study. In his home. Claiming the piece was a fake.

His own survival had to outweighed any loyalties.

"Her name is Amber Ross," Jacque said. "She works in New York. At the Metropolitan Museum of Art. She's in restoration. I assumed…"

"You assumed her forgery would pass my analysis," the Russian said. "You were wrong."

Jacque raised his shaking hands. "Please. Please. I didn't know. I was fooled, too. Tricked. I will help you recover the authentic—"

The Russian jerked his chin. The large man with the knife slid it across Jacque's throat, so suddenly, so cleanly, Jacque didn't feel the cut at first. Not until he saw his own blood spurt out across is pants. He covered the deep slice, stumbling from his chair, terror washing through him. No. No! Not now. Not like this. He was supposed to retire to somewhere warm. The Italian Rivera. Greece. Somewhere with hot weather. Where people didn't ask may questions. With good food and wine. And plenty of sunshine. Where he would never be cold again.

He tried to speak. The gurgling noise that escaped all he could manage. Cold seeped through him. Colder than he'd ever been. Desperate, he reached for the fireplace mantel. Blood smeared into the carved antique wood, dark in the uneven light. He collapsed to the floor in front of the fire. The flickering firelight dimming as he stared. As the cold rushed through his limbs.

Anton Mikhailov stared down at the body as it finished shaking, as the blood leaked out across the polished hardwood floor, forming a dark mirror reflecting the fire's light. Waiting for some sense of satisfaction at having exacted at least a portion of his revenge. The feeling never materialized. There were still betrayers to punish.

"Clean it?" Victor said, replacing his gun in his shoulder holster beneath his tailored suit jacket.

Nikko stood silently, waiting for instructions as he wiped blood from his knife on a cloth he'd pulled from his pocket.

"Clean the scene. But leave the body there. A warning to others who would try to betray me."

"The forger?" Victor asked.

"She will be next."

The men ignored the giant orange tom cat as it scurried into the room, mewing softly as it settled beside the dead man.

TWO

AMBER ROSS CONSIDERED the small machine in the display case, debating with herself. Around her the new Da Vinci's Science and Engineering exhibit was busy with tourists and locals alike moving between glass covered cases, around the various artifacts of the scientific and artistic genius. Whispered conversations, a few giggles from a group of school kids on a fieldtrip, the occasional too-loud voice floated around behind her. A background hum she could mostly ignore. The high ceiling gallery had the overhead lighting set to a slightly dimmer illumination than the corridors outside the gallery, to add weight and ambiance to the exhibit.

A good choice. Most of the uplit displays gave Da Vinci's various inventions and sketches a glorious bit of drama. And Da Vinci had been nothing if not a dramatic bastard.

But Amber's primary focus was this one particular piece. A miniature model of Da Vinci's machine for grinding lenses that she'd worked weeks to restore. Or at least restore as much as was possible.

The way the curator had arranged the miniature machine in the display case wasn't…right. The section of it that she hadn't been able to properly restore needed to be hidden better. Maybe if she turned it to the left a little?

She glanced around the gallery. No one was looking. The docents and security were otherwise occupied. Technically, she wasn't supposed to touch items out on display. That wasn't her job. She just restored damaged art pieces, her specialty antique technological devices. But she'd had a soft spot for this particular piece. It had come to her with a lot of water damage to the wood and some of the pieces barely held together. She was really proud of the work she'd done on it. Except for that one tiny section she'd had to fudge a little to get it close enough to right. The internal gears, the crank handle, the upright circular sanding stone…all perfectly restored. Most of the wooden casing holding the device had been fully restored as well. But in that one corner near the back, the wood was still showing some warp, some faint staining. The fit in that corner wasn't exactly level, either, which gave the base a slight tilt.

And that tiny flaw was too easy to see.

She scanned the gallery again. No one was watching. She could just open the case and move the box. Just a little. The curator wouldn't mind. Not after the deed was done. Maybe.

She winced. She and Jameson Adams—two last names? Really?—didn't always see eye to eye on these things. But what was that saying? Better to take the punishment later than ask permission? Or something like that. Anyway.

With a final glance around, ensuring none of the staff were paying attention to her, she took out the key to the display she'd *acquired* from Adams and opened the case. No alarms. No one watching. She gave the miniature machine a little tweak. Moving it just so. Letting the overhead light catch the black-painted gears, and the wooden side of the housing cast a shadow across the flaw…

There! That was better.

A hand on her shoulder startled an embarrassingly squeaky

gasp from her. She spun, a guilty apology springing to her lips. Only to discover the apology would have been wasted.

She put a hand to her chest and snarled at Rick O'Neill's smug, cocky grin.

"You're too easy to sneak up on," he said, leaning in close to whisper, "for a notorious art forger."

"Shut up." She hurriedly relocked the display case. "And you're an asshole for sneaking up on me."

"Stealing now? I thought you approved of returning precious items to museums. Getting them out of the hands of private collectors. Returning them to their rightful countries of origin where possible. All that?"

"I do. I am not stealing." She glared at him, and tucked the purloined key into the pocket of her dress slacks. She wasn't currently stealing. This didn't count as a lie. She'd stolen the key hours ago. She gestured at the case. "I spent weeks restoring this piece. I was just…adjusting it."

"Right." His grin turned crooked and entirely too knowing.

She glared harder since she had absolutely nothing to feel guilty about.

Rick O'Neill, treasure hunter and antiques dealer, was a six-foot tall, walking, talking source of constant irritation for her. Unfortunately, he was also a handsome one, with light brown hair and green eyes and that sort of boyish charm that made many women flutter their lashes at him. Plenty of men fluttered at him, too. He wielded that charm so effortlessly she was always left feeling awkward and clumsy.

Feeling awkward and clumsy made her grumpy.

She stuffed her hands in her pockets and scowled at him. Then took her hands out of her pockets and folded them in front of her. Why didn't she know what to do with her hands? She put them in her pockets again.

Nothing to do with feeling guilty at being caught messing with one of the displays.

"Why are you here?" she snapped to hide her fidgeting and low-level guilt.

His too-charming grin fell away, and his expression turned intent.

She frowned, her heartbeat thumping harder. Realizing belatedly they weren't supposed to be meeting today. Especially at her place of—legitimate—work.

He glanced around the gallery, then stepped close. "Jacque is dead."

Her breath rushed out of her so fast it left her dizzy. She dropped her arms to her sides, awkward hands forgotten, and took a step backward. Only avoided knocking into the display case because Rick caught her arm.

"Jacque is…" She met Rick's gaze. "How? Who?"

"How…better left unsaid."

She shivered and his hand on her arm flexed.

"Who…" A muscle in his jaw jumped. "The Russian."

Her heart gave a harsh lurch. "But that means—"

"He knows."

"You think Jacque actually—"

"Told him your name and where you work. He absolutely did."

"Then we're—"

"Fucked, yes."

She put a hand to her mouth as she swallowed hard. This was not good. This was very very bad.

"You swore to me no one would know," she hissed, stepping closer to him so they wouldn't be overheard and ignoring the fact that he smelled really good. How the hell could he smell so good at a time like this? At the very least he could have the decency to not smell at all.

"I didn't think he'd be able to figure it out," he said, his voice also low. "No one's seen the—" He cut off abruptly and leaned away from her as a group of teenage girls passed close enough to overhear the conversation.

One of the girls batted her lashes at Rick, and the others around her giggled, whispering to each other as they stared up at him.

Amber rolled her eyes. Like they had time for this. "Yes, yes, he's handsome," she said to the girls. "We all know." She made a shooing motion with her hands. "Move along."

Rick gave her a little smile. "You think I'm handsome."

"Shut up. What do we do now?"

Anton Mikhailov, also known simply as the Russian, was a notoriously violent billionaire collector, among other "hobbies" it was safest not to discuss. Or even mention. Those who crossed him ended up dead in very unpleasant ways. He was particularly dangerous when he didn't get what he wanted. She would never have taken the job, never even attempted to reproduce the pulse rate machine if she thought Jacque was going to sell it to Mikhailov. No one in their right mind sold *fakes* to the Russian.

"I can't believe I'm going to say this," Rick said, "But we have to get the…device. The real one. And hope that gives us some bargaining power."

"Get the device?" She blinked at him. "Just like that. Get the device? Are you insane?" Her voice rose as the shock got the best of her.

She snapped her mouth shut when a middle-aged man standing at the next display case frowned at them. Having this conversation out in public made her skin itch.

"Let's walk."

THREE

AMBER AND RICK left the exhibition gallery for one of the Metropolitan Museum's long corridors on the first floor, passing through the statue garden where the old section of the museum met the new and the brick walls of the old museum were still visible and beautifully preserved.

"No one knows where pulse rate machine is," she whispered, her voice harsh. "No one even knows for sure what it even looks like. That's why Jacque needed a forgery. Find the device." Rick had lost his mind. "What are we going to do?" She was trying not to let the panic overwhelm her. But her heartbeat was pounding out a rough rhythm against her ribs.

"I have a plan," he said.

"The last plan you had was for me to forge a priceless artifact and let Jacque sell it to the Russian."

"A mistake in hindsight. I thought it would be fine."

She glared at him.

"It will be fine," he assured. "We just need to get the real relic is all."

"Is all? Is all?" Her voice jumped to a loud squeak, drawing a glare from a woman standing in front of a Psyche and Eros statue. Amber dropped her voice back to a whisper. "That device hasn't been seen for centuries. Rumors and myths and *nothing*. For centuries. It might not even exist anymore. How the hell do you think we can find it before the Russian finds us? Especially since he's probably already here somewhere."

Suddenly, being out in the open in the middle of the museum seemed like a bad idea.

She fast-walked through the Medieval Art displays and into the American Wing, passing glorious Tiffany glass windows and the Arms and Armor gallery. At the back of the spacious room, near the wall of windows looking out onto Central Park, the café filled the huge, bright space with a background scent of coffee that normally made her thirsty. She was so worried now, the smell turned her stomach.

"Okay," Rick said, keeping pace with her easily. Which was annoying. "I have something I have to tell you. Promise not to get mad."

"Oh, it's too late. I'm already planning your murder. As we speak. I've even picked out a weapon."

He gave her a look. Then a resigned shrug. "Fine. But wait to kill me until after I've saved your life."

"Fair enough. Keep talking."

They reached the solid metal door that led back into one of the employee-only sections of the Museum. Amber took her keycard out of her pocket, ignoring the display case key in the same pocket, and swiped the card through the lock. As she started to enter her keycode into the panel next to the door, Rick cursed.

"Hurry."

She punched in the code, twisted the door handle, and looked past Rick to see what had him suddenly so anxious.

Two large men in dark suits and ties were walking through the bright, sunny statuary gallery, heading in their direction. The guns tucked beneath their suit jackets were frighteningly obvious when you knew what to look for.

Shit.

She and Rick swung inside, and she pulled the door closed tight behind her.

"Did they see us?" she asked, trying to slow her pulse and failing miserably. How the hell had the Russian's thugs gotten into the museum with guns? She'd had to get special permission to handle the fifteenth century crossbows she'd worked on two months ago.

"No idea." Rick grabbed her shoulders. "Let's move. Is there a back way out of here?"

"Gotta get my bag first."

"Time?"

"Making it. Can't go back to my apartment now."

Since finding out Jacque wanted the forged pulse rate machine to sell to the Russian—something she'd only found out about *after* she'd made it and handed it over to Rick to give to Jacque—she'd been bringing a go-bag with her to work every day. Just in case. It had some clothes, cash in a few currencies, two different sets of alias identification, and two backup burner cellphones.

That very morning, she'd been thinking she could drop the paranoid habit. Just that very morning. Thinking she could leave the bag at home and bring an ordinary purse into work instead of hauling the oversized backpack she pretended was a purse. A little over a week had passed. If the Russian had suspected a forgery, wouldn't he have acted sooner?

That's what she got for assuming.

"Had to sell to the Russian," she muttered as she led Rick along the brightly lit corridor to her restoration room. Her low heels clicked rapidly over the linoleum floors. "Had to give a notoriously evil collector a forged piece of history."

"Complain later. Get out of here now."

Inside the restoration room, painters worked at cleaning old works of art, carefully removing years of grime with painstaking precision, delicate with the priceless pieces. The room smelled of dust and turpentine and paint. Home away from home.

Her small room off the main restoration area was a little different. Table saws and sanding blocks. Chisels and planers and other tools neatly arrayed on hooks on one wall. Shelves filled with nails, screws, clamps, metal ties, stains and brushes. Piles of wood were stacked against the wall. And the delicate fifteenth century clock she was currently restoring for the museum sat on her workbench waiting to be finished.

She sighed as she grabbed her bag from the small locker at the back of the room. She wouldn't get to finishing restoring the clock now. Someone else, someone with less experience probably, would take over the job.

Maybe she could get out of this and still have her job when she got back. She might not be able to finish the clock, but maybe she didn't have to give up the life she'd built here.

"Hurry," Rick said, waving a hand at her from the doorway. "They won't be slowed down by card swipes and employee-only signs."

She shoved her arms through her backpack straps, set the key she'd stolen from Director Adams on her workbench, and led Rick to the exit at the rear of the museum which took the employees out into Central Park.

"Where are we going?" she asked as the early spring sunshine hit her face. She blinked against the glare and scanned the park.

Trees, fresh cut grass, a hint of horse manure and city traffic. Some people sitting under a tree on a blanket. A handful of women with strollers walking down a path toward the playground beside the museum.

No sign of Mikhailov's men. Yet.

"First stop," Rick said, "Italy."

Despite the dangers, a tingle of excitement ran through her. "Italy?"

Rick gave her a look. "No new shoes."

FOUR

VICTOR STEPPED onto the large marble stairs outside of the museum's main entrance, his gaze sweeping the gathered tourists sitting on the staircase soaking up sunshine. Traffic along Fifth Avenue was busy. Caricature artists and poster sellers did a brisk business along the tree-lined sidewalk in front of the museum. The ice cream cart had a line even though the early spring day was cool. The hot dog food truck had a line, too.

He nodded to his companion, and they walked down the stairs to the limo parked across the avenue on 83rd Street.

He carefully kept his expression neutral when the limo's darkly tinted window rolled down, releasing a puff of his employer's favorite cigar smoke.

"Anything?"

"She's gone," he told his boss. "The people we asked say they don't know where she's gone."

He held himself perfectly still, at attention, hands folded in front of him, as his boss absorbed the news. Failure, even to gather information, was always dangerous. Especially when his boss was in a mood for revenge. Victor had worked with him for two decades. He was as loyal to Anton Mikhailov as any of the men.

But he was careful not to take his position for granted. Or assume his boss wouldn't have him killed for failure.

Which meant he tried never to fail.

"One of the restoration artists thinks she saw Ross and a man leave through the back of the museum," he said.

"Rick O'Neill?"

"Likely. Description matched."

"Good."

"By the time we got around, they were gone." Victor carefully controlled his expression when his boss snarl. He didn't so much as flinch. A flinch would draw the wrong kind of attention.

"Tell our people at JFK and Newark to contact me immediately when they arrive."

"We can't take them at an airport, boss," Victor's companion, Nikko said.

Mikhailov gave him a look. Nikko shut up. Quickly.

"You think they won't drive or take a train to a different airport?" Victor asked. "Maybe DC?"

"They're in a hurry." The boss rolled his cigar between his fingers and considered the faintly glowing tip. His dark eyes narrowed, his expression shadowed in the dim interior of the limo. "They'll get on a plane as soon as they can."

"Any idea where they're headed, boss?" Nikko asked, his tone more deferential this time.

"Italy."

FIVE

SPRING FILLED Florence with warmth and light. The narrow streets and beautiful stone buildings lining the Arno River left Amber feeling almost nostalgic for a holiday she wasn't here to take. This time of year, the water in the river was high, so the smell was vaguely musty but not bad. And the warm sunshine more than made up for the perpetual honking of tiny cars and speeding mopeds whooshing past.

She loved Florence. The food. The galleries. The people.

The shoes.

"No," Rick said at the first boutique they passed. "We're here to keep you alive, not buy shoes."

Still. New shoes would have been nice. If she had to be killed, she'd prefer her corpse be found wearing fabulous heels rather than the serviceable tennis shoes she had on at the moment.

The Museo Galileo, located just past the Uffizi Gallery along the river, had a long line of tourists waiting outside the castle-like wooden doors. Amber sighed and headed for the line, but Rick took her arm.

"We go around the back."

"Are you going to tell me why we're here? I know the pulse rate machine isn't in the museum. Everyone in the art world would know if that mythical Galilean invention was here."

Mostly because scholars and art historians assumed it didn't exist.

During his last years, while on house arrest in his villa in Arcetri, Galileo Galilei's first biographer, and one of his many disciples, Vincenzo Viviani, recorded a story of Galileo inventing the first ever apparatus for accurately measuring the pulse rate after observing the pendulum swing of a lamp on a long chain in a cathedral in Pisa. Most modern scholars considered the story a fiction, made up by an eager Viviani to praise his master. Not least because the supposed lamp fixture wasn't installed in that particular church until four years after Galileo had moved away from Pisa.

But stories of the pulse rate machine had been circulating among rare artifacts collectors since not long after Galileo died.

The rumors traced the artifact through different private collections until the nineteenth century, when it disappeared from even rumor for more than a hundred years.

But during World War II, when museums and private collections across Europe were looted by the Nazis, rumors of Galileo's pulse rate machine resurfaced. There were no visual records of it. Only a few verbal descriptions in a handful of diaries from the seventeenth century. And no solid evidence, that she'd ever seen, to attest to the device having survived the scourges of time.

If it had ever really existed.

"The museum could have it hidden in a back room," Rick said.

She rolled her eyes. "And if that were the case, the Russian would have bought it from them by now."

"You think the museum would have sold it to him?"

"Not voluntarily."

Rick grunted.

She wasn't sure if that was agreement or not. She decided it was agreement.

He led her to a small gate behind the museum and into a narrow stone courtyard. Ivy grew up the yellow stucco wall of the apartment building at the rear of the courtyard. A weathered stone well in the center of the yard was surrounded by weeds, the wrought iron crank above it rusted and ancient looking. A breeze blew in from the river, bringing a musty tang and making the shadows beneath the buildings cold.

Rick led her to the ivy-covered wall and a thick wooden door half hidden behind the vines. "The pulse rate machine isn't here, obviously," he said, keeping his voice low.

"Then explain why we're here."

"You'll see."

He'd been telling her that since they'd left the car parking lot at JFK. "I hate you."

He grinned.

A small, balding man in wire frame glasses, wearing dark suit trousers and a dark suit vest over his white shirtsleeves, answered Rick's knock. He adjusted his glasses as he stared up at Rick, frowning slightly. Then his expression opened and he smiled.

"Rick O'Neill! It's been years," the man said, his English heavily accented. "What are you doing here? Have you brought me something interesting?"

"Giuseppe. Good to see you. This is my associate, Amber Ross. Amber, Giuseppe Martolli, Director of Special Collections at the Museo Galileo. May we come in?"

The small man gave Amber a brief once over, frowning now, a series of deep groves forming in his expansive forehead. Behind the glasses, his dark eyes narrowed. He tugged once at his short beard, then stepped aside.

"Come in. Come in." He closed the heavy wooden door behind them, then slid several solid looking bolt locks into place.

Amber considered the size of those locks. And the number of them. Five. Five large, heavy-duty bolt locks. No technology. No swipe cards or code panels. Just big, solid metal locks on a big, heavy oak door.

Old school. She approved.

Giuseppe waved for them to follow. "Come, we'll have a coffee and you can explain."

Since Amber was still groggy from the overnight flight, and they hadn't stopped for food or coffee on the way here, she nearly groaned in relief. After she'd gotten over her initial shock of knowing the Russian was looking for her, her appetite had returned. And her need for caffeine had surged.

Giuseppe led them into a small, dim room, lit by a single overhead bulb and the shadowed daylight creeping in from a high window. The room held a table covered in books, two wooden chairs, and a second, smaller table with a small hotplate and a stainless steel stove top espresso maker sitting on it.

A tiny shelf over the second table revealed an impressive array of small ceramic espresso cups. Giuseppe poured out one for Amber first, handing it to her with a little smile, before giving one to Rick with a less cordial expression.

The strong, rich scent made her sigh. The first sip gave her life.

"Now," Giuseppe said, leaning against the larger, book-covered table, his arms crossed over his chest. "Tell me what you're here for."

"I need to see the pendulum," Rick said.

Amber kept her expression hidden in her cup. Pendulum?

"Why?" Giuseppe asked.

Rick sighed. "I have to go get it." He made a face. "The Russian is looking for it."

"I know," Giuseppe said. "He's been here multiple times.

During the last visit, he claimed Jacque had a lead on procuring it. I thought…" Giuseppe raised thick brows and tilted his head toward Rick.

"I would never sell it to Mikhailov," Rick said. "It's still where it's been all these years. As far as I know."

"There have been…rumors."

"Jacque's dead, Giuseppe," Rick said.

The small man straightened, blinking a few times behind his wire rims. "The Russian."

Rick nodded.

"You have…something to do with this, yes?"

"Not with Jacque's death." Rick scowled.

Giuseppe lifted his hands in a claiming gesture "No, no. I'm not asking about that. I'm asking about what's brought you here."

Rick glanced at Amber. She shrugged. It wasn't like the most dangerous criminal on the planet didn't already know about her. A curator at the Galileo Museum was hardly a bigger threat.

"Jacque sold Mikhailov a…a replica."

"Of Galileo's pulse rate machine? How? Where did he get something like that?"

Rick nodded to Amber. She lifted her cup and gave a little finger salute.

"You…" Giuseppe looked between her and Rick. "You created a replica?"

"I did."

"Based on what? There are no visual records."

"I used some diary entries from his daughter Virginia, Sister Maria Celeste, and some of Viviani's writings not included in the official biography, as well as a few diary entries from Galileo's time in Padua, written by Sagredo. Combined those details." She shrugged. "I'm very good with fifteenth, sixteenth, and seventeenth century technology." She made a little face, feeling defensive. "It was an excellent…replica."

"Not a replica if sold as if the original," Giuseppe pointed out. "Those are called forgeries."

"Same skill set," she said, pursing her lips primly.

"Hmm. It was good enough to fool the Russian?"

"For a week," Rick answered. "I'm not sure how he discovered it wasn't authentic."

"It's not like there's anything to compare it to," Amber muttered. She'd love to know how Mikhailov figured it out, too. She wasn't sure why. Professional pride, maybe. She'd put in a lot of work into ensuring that particular...replica looked authentic.

Giuseppe frowned a little, then asked, "Why do you wish to recover it now? After all these years?"

"I need some bargaining power," Rick said. "I don't want to hand it over to him. I promised your father if I ever went after it, I'd ensure it came back to the museum. But..." Rick glanced at her. "Mikhailov knows Amber's the person who...created the replica."

"Ah." Giuseppe nodded. His glasses slipped down his long nose, and he pushed them up again with a single finger to the nose bridge. "In that case." He gestured for them to set their cups down. "This way."

Amber gulped the last of her espresso shot and looked longingly at the kettle. No time for more.

Survive first. Espresso later.

SIX

ANTON MIKHAILOV SAT in his limo down the block from the Museo Galileo, one street away from the river. He watched the tourists walking past, their faces in their phones as they attempted to navigate the Florentine streets. The radio in the limo was tuned to a Champions League match between Juventus and Real Madrid, but he barely paid attention.

His thoughts were of things bloodier than soccer matches.

Victor and Nikko slid into the limo a few moments later.

"Well?"

"They went inside," Victor said. "The little man, the director, Giuseppe Martolli. He let them in."

Anton looked out the window, deep in thought, rolling his unlit cigar between his fingers.

"You want us to go get them, boss?" Nikko asked.

He faced his two most loyal men.

Victor had been with him for…twenty years. He could count on him to maintain his composure and not get distracted easily. He was quick and efficient, focused. A good leader of the other men. Nikko was younger. Deadlier. But not a great strategic thinker. He was a soldier. A very loyal soldier. But not a captain.

Not a general. While Anton might trust Victor with elements of strategy, he would never pass such a responsibility to Nikko.

"Why would we stop them now?" he asked. "When they'll lead us to the real relic."

"They are going after it, then," Victor said.

"Why else come to Martolli."

"We're going to follow them."

He smiled faintly at Victor. "We're going to follow them." Anton put his unlit cigar in his mouth, nodding in satisfaction. The first sense of satisfaction he'd felt since discovering Jacque had sold him a fake.

He'd been planning this for a long long time. And he would not let his revenge slip through his fingers.

Allowing O'Neill and Ross to lead him to the relic would save him a lot of trouble. After Jacque's failure, he'd intended on simply forcing Martolli to hand over the pendulum before killing him. But Anton didn't know how to *use* the pendulum to find the map. A final, missing piece he hadn't been able to uncover. It would take him time and money and blood to find the real artifact on his own.

He was unconcerned with the money or the blood. It was the time… He no longer had the time. If he had, he'd have continued his own research and not relied on Jacque.

But Kalashnik would be untouchable soon. Jacque had delayed Anton enough. There was no more time to waste.

Now, Rick O'Neill and Amber Ross would lead him right to his prize. Easy. Neat.

Kalashnik would not escape him. He would get the relic.

And his revenge.

SEVEN

GIUSEPPE LED them down a long stone-walled corridor to narrow stairs that descended to a basement level. The temperature dropped significantly with each step, making Amber miss the warm sunshine outside.

The bottom of the stairs opened on small foyer and a sealed arched wooden door. The door looked ancient. The tiled floor and white stucco walls also showed signs of age and some water damage.

Lifting a heavy key from inside the pocket of his suit vest, Giuseppe opened the thick wooden door on hinges that surprisingly didn't squeak. A rush of dry, cold air puffed out as the door revealed a dark interior.

The small man turned and stared at Rick. "You may look at the pendulum, but I will not allow it to leave the museum. That's what *I* promised my father."

"That's all I need," Rick said.

Giuseppe held his gaze for a long minute before leading them into the room.

Once inside, Amber realized it wasn't completely dark. There were dim overhead lights that flickered on as they came into the room, but most of the illumination came from floor lights that cast weirdly dancing yellow shadows on an arched stone roof.

The room was downright cold. But the air was dry with a vague undertone of aging parchment and preservation formulas. Amber breathed in the various scents of old things, feeling instantly at home. She loved old things.

And she loved this storage room. Filled with cases and cases of antique objects and devices. There were maps, reams of parchment inside leather folios, several models of different versions of the universe, a number of clocks, and at least four different telescopes. Leather bound books and folios lines shelves covering one wall. And racks of transportation crates for paintings leaned against the other. At the back of the room, just visible through all the delightful clutter, another door.

Here, for the first time, signs of modern technology. This door was a dark gray metal that reminded her of a bank vault. Beside it a panel with both biometric and traditional code entry locks.

Giuseppe paused at the panel, taking in a deep breath. "I have not had cause to open this door in some time," he murmured, almost to himself. "Not since my father passed last year at least."

"I'm sorry for your loss," Amber said quietly. She'd had a complicated relationship with her parents. But when they'd died, she'd felt that ache of grief for years after. Still felt it when she got sentimental.

"Thank you," Giuseppe said, smiling a little at her. He removed his glasses, then set his hand on the palm scanner and his eye to the retinal scanner. After putting his glasses back on, he punched a series of numbers into the panel. He covered his actions by turning his back to Rick.

Rick rolled his eyes and shook his head.

She didn't blame Giuseppe, though. She wouldn't trust Rick

with that code either. Even if he couldn't replicate the palm and retinal print.

A hiss of releasing air, then the huge steel door swung outward.

Lights inside blinked on, brighter than the rest of the storage room, bright enough she had to squint against the initial glare.

Inside, the resemblance to a bank vault continued. The small room was encased in steel, with several tall, dark gray metal cabinets with closed drawers taking up the center of the space. Nothing was labeled, and each drawer and cabinet looked identical.

She stepped close to the nearest one to study the small panels in the center of each drawer.

"More biometrics?" she asked.

"One can never be too careful with certain relics," Giuseppe said.

He walked to the rear of the vault, to one of the cabinets farthest from the door. Nothing here to indicate the contents of the drawers either. No numbers or letters or any other identifying markings to set this cabinet apart from any other. Giuseppe pressed his thumb against the lock panel on a middle drawer. It popped open just enough for him to hook his fingers into the sliding drawer and pull it the rest of the way out.

Inside, a meticulously maintained wooden box, cube shaped, roughly one foot by one foot. Based on the hinges and locking clip, and without being able to examine it more closely, Amber would say it dated from the eighteenth century. Not old enough to be something Galileo might have owned.

Giuseppe looked up and caught her frown. "The box came to store the pendulum much later than the pendulum was made."

She nodded but didn't comment. Especially since she didn't know what the pendulum was, exactly.

Giuseppe opened the lid on the box, without a key, folding the heavy top backward on well-oiled hinges to reveal a blue velvet-lined interior. On top of the velvet sat a large brass ball attached to a linked chain. The chain wrapped around the base of the ball, giving the whole thing a sort of Saturn look.

The brass ball was covered in symbols that reminded her of astrological charts, spots like stars or planets around concentric rings, and here and there a rendering of one of the constellations.

"It's beautiful," she murmured, her fingers hovering over the globe without touching it. "Galileo made this?"

"It was made in the Padua workshop, by Marcantonio Mazzoleni. At the direction of Galileo."

"For an experiment?" She couldn't look away. The exactness of the globe, the delicacy of the seams and the perfection of the etchings… Mazzoleni was a superb engineer. A real artist in his own right.

"Of a sort." Giuseppe smiled. Then he looked at Rick. "You're sure you can manage it? Without having the pendulum with you?"

"I'm sure," he said. "May I?" He nodded to the box, lifting his hands a little.

Amber stepped aside so Rick could take the baseball-sized pendulum from the box. He held it up by the chain, studying the etchings. With a slight wrist twitch, he set the heavy brass ball to swing gently in a tight circle.

He held it up for her. "You got this?" he asked.

She nodded and stared at the pendulum, watched it spin, studied the etchings herself, the way they moved as the pendulum swung. Memorizing.

One of the things that made her excellent at both restoration work and forgeries… She had an eidetic memory for three dimensional objects. Details, design, shapes and sizes, angles. All precisely imbedded in her memory after only a few minutes of study.

She touched the chain, near Rick's hand, and he passed the pendulum to her. She felt the weight, the perfect balance. She lowered the chain through her fingers another inch and watched the larger circuit made by the brass ball.

When she was satisfied she could replicate the pendulum, given the right equipment, she placed it back into the box, once again wrapping the chain around the circumference of the globe so that it resembled a brass-colored Saturn.

Giuseppe pursed his lips as he closed the lid and replaced the box in the drawer. He didn't ask any questions until he'd resealed the door and led them back out of the vault.

"That is…all you'll need here?" Giuseppe asked. "My father thought…"

"We've got what we need now," Rick said. He put a hand on Giuseppe's shoulder. "Be careful. The Russian might come looking for us here."

Giuseppe waved a hand, dismissing the warning. "More likely he will follow you. Be wary on this particular treasure hunt, Rick. Mikhailov is like a hunting dog, and you are the fox. If you aren't careful to cover your scent, you won't get far."

EIGHT

THE TRAIN to Venice wasn't particularly crowded, so Amber and Rick took a four block of seats with a table, making it easier to eat the sandwiches they'd picked up in the train station. The train stopped in Padua, so Amber had assumed that was their destination. She waited to ask questions, though, until they were well underway, with the Tuscan countryside flying past. Rolling landscapes of farmland and wineries, interspersed with modern cities, and the occasional picturesque Italian village.

"Why did I memorize that pendulum?" she murmured around her mozzarella and tomato sandwich, the thick focaccia bread a delicious salty contrast to the creamy cheese.

"It's better if I explain when we get to where we're going?"

"Padua?" That was one of the cities where Galileo had lived and taught at the university. He'd done some of his best work during his time in Padua, even though he was famous for, probably apocryphal, experiments in Pisa.

"Venice," Rick said.

She frowned when that was all he said. "I gave up shoe shopping for this. I'm gonna need more."

He sighed and looked around the train car. There were half a dozen other people. The closest were a young couple who were extremely into each other two rows in one direction, and an older Italian woman doing a video call as she knitted three rows in the opposite direction. No one close enough to hear their conversation over the sounds of the train zinging over the tracks.

Rick still leaned across the table to get that little bit closer to her. She mirrored his movement.

"You know how the rumors of the pulse rate machine resurfaced during the war? Well, turns out the Nazis did find it, buried amidst a private collection in Prague. One particular collector, a minor colonel, knew what it was and stole it from the collection for himself. At the end of the war, when the Nazis were fleeing justice for their war crimes, this colonel managed to get himself and his family out of Europe. With the pulse rate machine."

"So it's not in Europe? Why are we, then?"

Rick lowered his voice further, so it was almost impossible to hear. "The colonel's family were tracked down by the Israeli secret service. One of whom was married to a Galilean historian and was a bit of Galilean expert herself."

"Giuseppe's parents?" Amber guessed.

Rick nodded. "Essa also recognized the significance of the device this colonel had in his possession when he was captured. And she decided it was safer to leave it hidden."

That had Amber leaning back in her seat. "Why? Why wouldn't she want to bring it to the public if she knew what it was?"

"She felt…based on some documents kept with the artifact, that revealing its existence would be too dangerous?"

"Dangerous? It was built to measure pulse rates? Where in that is there danger?"

Granted, it was an invention Galileo never spoke of in his own writings. There had to be a reason he never claimed credit for its invention. When a Venetian physician created one in 1626,

Galileo didn't dispute his claim to have invented the first. Galileo was notorious for protecting his own providence on inventions and discoveries, on ensuring no one got credit for something he'd created or discovered first. But he didn't do that over the pulse rate machine.

This was why most modern scholars thought the device was a myth. If Galileo himself never mentioned it or tried to claim credit for it, they argued, it probably didn't exist and was just a story invented by his biographer.

"The real device doesn't *just* measure pulse rates," Rick said. "That's the problem. The reason Giuseppe's mother didn't bring it back to the museum."

"What the hell does it do?"

The door at the opposite side of the train car whooshed open, making it momentarily louder. A woman in a perfectly tailored, dark blue pants suit and fabulous nude heels strolled down the aisle, her dark hair pulled up in a neat bun. Her gaze skimmed over the other passengers, but zeroed in on Rick and Amber after only a moment.

She smiled slightly as she slid into the seat next to Amber without waiting for an invitation.

"Good afternoon," she said, her accent a funny combination of Italian and German. "Rick O'Neill."

Rick's return smile looked forced. Amber glanced at the woman again. She looked vaguely familiar but Amber couldn't seem to place her.

When Rick introduced her as Inspector Gail Haviard of Interpol, the familiarity dropped into place. Amber had never directly dealt with Inspector Haviard, but she'd escaped out from under her a few times.

"On another treasure hunt?" the inspector asked Rick.

"Just a little casual touristing with my girlfriend," Rick said.

Amber bit the inside of her cheek so she wouldn't react to that statement.

The inspector turned a little in her seat and smiled at Amber. "Amber Ross. Or is it Adele Winters now? Maybe Kelly Anders?"

Amber kept her smile carefully neutral. "Amber is fine. I don't believe we've met before Inspector."

"No. But I've encountered some of your work over the years. Good stuff. You're very talented."

"I am excellent at restorations," Amber said with a little nod. "It's nice to have one's work appreciated."

"Yes, the restorations are also very good." Inspector Haviard looked at Rick again. "You heard about Jacque?"

"I did. Terrible news."

"Quite."

"Do you know who?"

"We all do, don't we." She gave a little shrug. "But that individual has always been difficult to convict of anything. He owns too many politicians."

"Well, I wish you luck in your investigation," Rick said. "Be nice to have Jacque's killer brought to justice."

"It would," Haviard agreed with a little nod. She held Rick's gaze a bit longer. Then smiled. "Try to stay out of his way. I'd rather not walk into a flat to see your body sprawled out in a pool of blood, with only a cat sitting next to you as witness."

A muscle along Rick's jaw jumped. "Yeah, I'd prefer that, too."

She tilted her head when she looked back at Amber. "I suspect we'll meet again one day, Ms. Ross."

Not if Amber had any say in the matter. "That would be lovely," she said, with a forced smile. "Great shoes, by the way."

The inspector pushed her foot out into the aisle and glanced at the high heel. "Thank you. I like them, too." She gave Rick and Amber a nod before standing. But before she'd taken more than a step away, she shifted back and leaned over the table. "By the way, there are rumors circulating that the reason *he* killed

Jacque was that someone sold him a forged Galileo artifact. I don't suppose either of you knows anything about that?"

Amber felt like her face might crack under the strain of holding her neutral smile. "Someone sold the… sold *him* a forged piece? That doesn't seem very smart."

"It wasn't. A potentially deadly mistake." Haviard held Amber's gaze, her dark eyes boring into Amber like she could see her soul.

Amber didn't fidget or twitch her cheek, though she wanted to. She didn't glance away from the inspector's direct look when she said, "Definitely a huge mistake. But what can you do? People make mistakes all the time."

"Yes," Haviard said. "And it's my job to ensure there are consequences for those mistakes. If they break the law, of course."

"Of course," Amber said.

Haviard glanced from Amber to Rick. Her expression contemplative. "Well, then. I'll leave you to the rest of your journey. Enjoy…touristing? Padua, is it?"

"Yes," Rick lied without blinking. "Love the university there."

Haviard nodded as she straightened from the table. "I hear they have an excellent collection of Galileo artifacts, too."

"We'll have to check that out," Rick said.

They didn't speak again until the inspector had left the train car.

Amber scowled. "She knows about—"

"The pulse rate machine now. Yup."

"You think she'll try to—"

"Stop us? No." Rick faced her. "I think she'll follow us."

"Why? To retrieve the machine?"

Rick shook his head. "To catch the Russian when he tries to kill us."

NINE

VENICE IN SPRING was a lovely city. The canals were full and there was plenty of water movement, so the smells were well below the August sewer scents. Too many tourists pushed and shoved around the area off the train station and crowded the water buses. With Easter only a few weeks away, the city on the Aegean bustled with activity.

Bright sunshine painted the stucco walls and elegantly carved stone balconies. Flowers bloomed in containers hanging on window hooks, and laundry stretched across lines between buildings, above the stone pathways through the more residential areas.

Rick led Amber over several bridges, the dark green canal water below, to one of the islands farthest away from St Marco's Square and the majority of the day tourists.

Amber didn't precisely object to all the walking. She'd switched from her low work heels to a pair of easy-to-run-in tennis shoes when they'd reached JFK. The late afternoon was sunny and warm, the pedestrian traffic light. But the farther they walked, the more antsy she got. They were in a very residential area. And she was very aware of not being Venetian.

Standing out and being too obvious seemed like a bad idea when an international crime lord wanted you dead.

"You sure about this?" she murmured, her voice low as they passed down another narrow path, under enough laundry to provide some nice shade on the street. Her skin itched, like she was being watched.

"We're almost there. Do not bolt and run for the nearest shoe store."

"Do not joke about that at a time like this."

Because she was seriously considering bolting for the nearest shoe store—especially if there were lots of tourists. She could blend in with tourists.

He reached back and took her hand, giving it a squeeze, before releasing it. She did not trip over a paving stone. She was very proud of herself.

Seemingly at random, because she no longer knew where she was, Rick led them between buildings, down a narrow alley, into a tiny postage stamp-sized courtyard and up to a four-story building that looked generally like its neighbors. This one was painted a soft pink over the stucco and its windows were fronted by wrought iron railings with hanging boxes of flowers that managed to look colorfully full despite the excess of shade. Everything smelled of flowers and the pungent salty-fishy scent of the canal.

Questions piled up but she kept her mouth shut as Rick pressed a little buzzer beside the door. Long long moments passed before anyone answers.

Amber spent the wait checking behind her and scanning their surroundings. That sense of being watched still tingling along the back of her neck.

When the door opened, she jumped and then silently cursed herself. Fortunately, Rick didn't seem to notice. She'd never live that down.

A woman, probably in her eighties, stood behind the door.

She was ramrod straight, her thick gray hair styled into a rather attractive bob, her makeup light and impeccable. She wore a pair of dark brown slacks, cream button-down shirt, and the most fabulous pair of flats Amber had ever seen—brass-colored and decorated with dark studs. All together elegant and casual at once.

Amber decided in that instant she wanted to be the older woman when she grew up. At least to inhabit that look.

The woman's gaze danced over them, settled on Rick. Unlike Giuseppe, she didn't smile.

"You promised him you wouldn't go looking for it," she said, her accent light and sharp.

"I promised him *if* I did, it would go to the museum," Rick answered, not balking at the accusation.

"She didn't want it found."

"He was of two minds. May we come in?"

"I heard about Jacque and the forgery." Her gaze danced to Amber again. Her dark eyes were serious and steady behind her large, red-rimmed glasses. "And the Russian."

Amber wanted to shift from foot to foot and check behind her again. She held the woman's gaze instead. She had no idea why they were there. Rick hadn't finished his story on the train after the encounter with Inspector Haviard. They'd searched the table, seats, even their backpacks, for possible tracking and listening devices, and found nothing. But Rick still refused to talk anymore.

She couldn't blame him. But she would have liked to feel less awkwardly clueless in front of this particular Italian woman.

"Then you understand why it's better if we don't stay out here talking," Rick said when the woman still didn't let them in.

She pulled in a deep breath, her mouth pinched, but she nodded and stood to the side. Once she had the door closed behind them, she wordlessly led them past an old-fashioned elevator with the sort of door that had to be manually opened and closed and toward the back of the house.

Amber stopped next to the elevator to admire it. She never worked on things this big, but she appreciated the marvel of it. The intricate wrought iron details, the wooden shelf inside, the red carpeted floor, the combination of old and the new, a little warn but still beautiful… Loved it. No one took the time to make useful things beautiful anymore.

Rick took her arm and pulled her away from the elevator, but she went reluctantly.

The woman, whom Rick hadn't introduced yet—another difference from their meeting with Giuseppe—led them through the building, around a corner, and into a huge workshop, the entire back of which opened onto a mid-sized canal. Across the canal, a small, tree-lined park and a few more apartment buildings. Several motorboats puttered past. The dock just outside of the workshop had a single motorboat moored to it bobbing gently in the wash from other boats.

The workshop itself was obviously set up for metallurgy work. Stacks of raw sheet metal, hot forges, wracks of hooks and long sticks. There were some pieces of dark wood here and there. And a work bench with tiny gears scattered around an elegant looking device whose use Amber couldn't immediately discern. Which only made her want to get closer and investigate.

But Rick was still holding her arm, which prevented her from wandering off through the shop.

Probably for the best.

The woman turned her back to the canal, which for some reason left Amber edgy, and said, "I don't approve of this. You should know that. Galileo himself wanted this piece forgotten. One of the reasons Essa hid it."

"But he didn't destroy it," Rick said. "Neither did she. It's a piece of history."

"And unscrupulous individuals will pay a lot, and kill many, to get it. It's better off remaining where it is."

"You won't help?"

"I promised Essa I would help Bertolo if he came to me. And he asked me to help you in his stead." Her mouth pursed again. "I will help. But I felt my objections should be noted."

"And they are. Thank you."

She huffed. "Thank me? You should probably be cursing me."

Rick flashed her one of his most charming smiles, one he'd kept under wraps until that moment. Amber watched in awe as the woman softened, her expression turning wry instead of pinched. She rolled her eyes at him, but some color crept into her cheeks.

"You should be criminally charged for that smile," the woman said, shaking her head. "Put that away. You have work to do."

Amber folded her lips into her mouth so she wouldn't laugh.

TEN

AMBER STARED AT THE SEAL, sunlight streaming in off the canal glinting on its dark copper face and designs. Set into the brown tile floor near one wall of the large workshop, the seal looked like a marker, the kind of plaque that recorded historic houses or historic spots on a sidewalk. The sort of thing tourists stopped to look at sometimes, but most locals forgot was there.

Diona Simionato, who'd finally introduced herself, had directed Rick and Amber to push aside the heavy metal shelves and boxes covering the seal, the metal scrapping loudly across the tiles. Then she gestured at it with a little flip of her hand.

Circular and about two feet in diameter. A few bumps and valleys here and there. There were some lines and dots circling the perimeter, moving concentrically inward. The central inscription, mostly in Latin, said something about metalwork being the laboring heart of the gods, except heart was writing in Spanish instead of Latin or Italian. The patterns inscribed in the seal seemed abstract and more for texture than to create a picture of anything. It was a nice looking piece, but nothing about it would draw undue attention.

Amber only noticed the silence that had grown around her after several minutes of studying the seal.

"Well?" Rick said.

She blinked and looked at him. "Well, what?"

"The pendulum?"

She frowned. "Huh?"

Diona put her hands on her hips and gave Rick a look. "Giuseppe wouldn't let you take the pendulum. You do not have it."

"No," Rick said. "I don't need it."

"You cannot open the seal without it." She shrugged. "Shame. I suppose the treasure will remain hidden. As Essa wanted."

"We need it to save Amber's life. So no, it won't remain hidden."

Amber winced at the reminder. "I'm missing something, aren't I?"

"The pattern on the pendulum," Rick said. "Essa used it when designing the seal. That pattern holds the key to unlocking this."

She mirrored Diona's gesture, putting her hands on her hips as she stared at him. "You know, you could have mentioned that. Out loud. At some point. In the last few minutes. Or the last few hours. Or even…just now. When mentioning the pendulum."

"I thought you'd get it," he said.

"That was an insult, wasn't it? You just insulted me."

"Never. I was complimenting you."

She snorted.

"Children, I have other things to do," Diona said. "I have a commission to complete. Either you finish why you're here, or you leave."

Several boats motored by on the canal, the sounds echoing in the open workshop. When the noise died down, Rick said, "From what Bertolo told me, the pendulum *pattern* is the key to opening the seal. Not the pendulum itself."

"And you know the way that all works," Amber said. "Right?"

"You're the one with the eidetic memory."

"I know what the pendulum looks like. I don't know how to use the patterns to open the seal."

Rick scowled and gestured at the copper circle. "You haven't been trying. Try."

She opened her mouth. Snapped it closed. Pointed a finger at him as she sucked in a deep breath through her nose. Another motorboat zoomed past, its wake slapping against the dock outside the workshop. The salty breeze off the water cooled her cheeks, but not her temper.

Shaking her head, she removed her backpack and dropped it on the floor next to his. Then she squatted down to study the copper seal closer.

Without looking up, she asked Diona, "Would you happen to have a piece of paper and pencil I could borrow?"

"You can't write down what's on the pendulum," Rick said. "No pictures. No replicas. Giuseppe insisted on it because his mother insisted on it. I would have just taken a photo otherwise."

Amber tilted her head to one side, looking at the seal from a slightly different angle, her eyes narrowed. Absently, she said, "I'm not going to draw the pendulum. I just need to…work something out." And she was better at working things out with her hands moving.

Diona left and returned a few moments later, handing Amber a sturdy sketch book and a sharpened graphite pencil. The tools of an artist. She thanked the older woman, then sat down on the tile floor and started sketching out the bumps and dots on the seal.

When she looked at it from the right angle, the pattern

reminded her of the celestial pattern on the pendulum. The way the lines intersected with some of the dots that could be stars or planets. She closed her eyes as she remembered the pendulum, the details, the exact places of those dots. The way the images of the constellations had also sat at exact spots along the etched lines encircling the pendulum's globe shape.

When she opened her eyes, facing the seal, the pattern started to emerge. That ridge at just the same place as a constellation. That little dot in just the same place as this starburst. Where the pendulum had multiple rings circling it from pole to pole, running through the three-dimensional shape, with multiple points like planets and stars etched on different levels, the seal had multiple rings moving from the outer edge to the interior where the Latin inscription was.

She moved her pencil over the paper without looking at what she was drawing, instead stared at the seal while holding the pendulum image in her mind. She let the pencil circle and circle on the page as she mentally fit the etched lines on the pendulum with the lines on the seal.

Not in an obvious order. Not from pole to pole. Each line matched, though. Seven on the pendulum. Seven on the seal. The points were spread farther apart on the seal. The constellations on the pendulum seemed to be represented on the seal as faint ridges and depressions.

Her hand stopped on the page.

Ah!

Two motorboats crossed paths outside, their combined wake sloshing against the workshop's dock. A seagull landed on one of the dock's pilings and squawed loudly. The late afternoon breeze filled the workshop with a seaweed smell from the canal. All a perfectly ordinary background hum to her epiphany.

Amber stared hard at the rings on the seal. Yes.

"You have something?" Rick asked, squatting down next to her.

"The dots on the pendulum match the dots on the rings around the seal. But the way they line up, the outer line on the seal is the circumference line on the pendulum. And they go back and forth as they move inward so that the inner two lines on the seal are the pole points on the pendulum."

Rick nodded. "And that means?"

"That I know how the pendulum and seal line up," she said, scowling at the side of his face. "Like I just said."

"But how do we open the seal?"

"Not even a cookie for figuring the lines out? Rude." She tapped the pencil against the sketchbook as she ran her gaze along the dots. The way they lined up on the seal not an exact match to the way they lined up on the pendulum.

But if she moved that line on the seal an inch to the left… And then slid that one a little the other direction… And the middle one had to be just there…

She grinned, tapped a few more times against the sketchbook. Yes. "Pa bump pa bump pa bump…" She glanced at Rick and raised her brows. "Like a heartbeat."

He frowned.

"What? I thought you'd get it." She mimicked his earlier comment to her.

Diona laughed. "I hope you can keep her alive," she said to Rick. "I find I might like her."

"Thank you." Amber grinned at Rick.

"Explain what you've found. We're running out of time."

He was right. Shame, though. She would've liked to have gloated longer.

"The pattern from the pendulum, that's reproduced here, isn't lined up exactly like it is on the pendulum, but with a few movements it can be."

"I'm not seeing it," Rick said.

She set aside the sketchbook and moved onto her knees,

ignoring the uncomfortably hard tile surface as the excitement filled her. "Look."

She moved the outer edge of the seal by putting her finger into one of the dots and circling it to the left. The movement was remarkably smooth, a sign of work done by a real craftsperson. She met Rick's gaze and grinned. He motioned her to finish.

Starting from the outside and working her way inward, she turned each circle around the edge of the seal until she'd realigned them precisely the way they lined up on the pendulum.

When she had the last two lines in the center of the seal aligned to match the small circles that had moved around the poles of the globe, she took a breath.

"Where does that 'pa bump' thing come in?" Rick asked.

She pointed to the inscription. "Corazón instead of the Latin cor or the Italian cuore."

He nodded. "The rest is in Latin. I missed that. But…what does it mean?"

"Heart. You know. Pulse rate machine. Heart…"

He gave her a look. "I know what corazón means. I'm asking about the seal." He nodded at the copper circle. "It's still, you know, sealed."

Amber sighed. "So impatient."

She pressed the "heart," where it was ingeniously placed at the very center of the inscription, the raised lettering rough against her fingertips.

A hiss of released air.

The seal lifted vertically, on hydraulic legs, revealing a narrow cavity beneath.

Rick laughed. "I can't believe she created this."

"Essa was a genius," Diona said.

"Yeah she was," Amber agreed, with feeling.

Rick reached into the cavity, pulling out a flat leather pouch.

Another motorboat puttered past the open workshop, the engine almost silent as it moved slowly by.

The quieter engine, unlike all the noisy engines passing previously, made Amber look up.

In time to see a man with a very large machine gun pointed right inside the workshop.

ELEVEN

THE RATATATAT SPRAY of bullets ricocheted through the workshop, clanging off metal, thumping into wood. Glass on the workbench shattered. Pieces of tile exploded around them.

Rick grabbed Diona and pulled her behind the metal shelves he and Amber had moved earlier. Amber scrambled for cover behind the shelves on her hands and knees, dragging hers and Rick's backpacks with her.

The shelves were stacked with thick wooden boxes, all full of scrap metal, but she wasn't so sure those boxes would hold up to the hail of bullets for very long.

"My workshop," Diona groaned. "Bastards. Who are they? The Russian's men? I will kill them. I will kill them with my bare hands."

Obviously, pissing off an Italian woman was a bad idea. Amber could relate, though. The workshop had been magnificent and now it was a bullet riddled disaster. She wanted to cry. Well, she wanted to survive the hail of gunfire first. Then she'd bemoan Diona's loss.

"We have to get out of here," Rick shouted above the noise. "Back way?"

"The deliver door." Diona waved a hand to a large metal door not far behind them, opposite the door they'd come through to get into the workshop.

"They may have that covered," Amber warned. She slipped her backpack back on, tossed Rick's to him, then looked around for the leather packet they'd pulled from beneath the seal.

Horrified to see it laying out in the open where Rick had dropped it when he'd grabbed Diona.

"Shit."

She took her backpack back off again and squatted low to the floor, trying to gauge the gunfire.

"What the hell are you doing?" Rick said.

"We can't leave without whatever's in that packet."

"Stay here. I'll get it."

She didn't give him a chance to argue further. Keeping as low to the ground as she could get, she scrambled forward, snatched the leather packet and scrambled backward like a crab so she could watch the swing of the machine gun.

Tile pieces flew up from where she'd been, one sharp piece catching her cheek before she made it back behind the shelves.

She touched her fingers to the cut. A little blood, but nothing too bad.

"If you ever do something like that to me again, I will kill you myself," Rick said.

"Stop. You'll make me think you love me." She put her backpack back on. "Let's get out of here."

"What happens if they are watching the door?" Diona asked, not unreasonably.

"We'll know in a minute."

In the distance, Amber heard the sound of a siren.

The hail of bullets didn't slow even a little bit. Guess they weren't worried about the police catching them.

That probably wasn't a good sign.

Amber, Diona, and Rick stuck close to the wall, keeping

shelves and boxes between them and the open side of the workshop as they reached the delivery door. It was a large metal door that rolled upward and was wide enough for a small cart or truck to back in through.

"Don't lift it fully yet," Rick said, still shouting over the racket caused by lots and lots of bullets clanging off lots and lots of metal. "Part way, see if anyone takes the bait."

"And if they do?" Diona said as she pressed the door lift button.

"Then we find another way out," Rick said.

Diona stopped the door when it was a foot up off the ground, revealing the stone walkway beyond.

No bullets. No shouting.

The sound of approaching sirens and more motorboats got louder. The gunfire died suddenly and a revving engine followed.

Amber's ears rang from all the noise, and then all the sudden ceasing of noise.

She barely heard Rick when he said, "I think we're good. Let's go."

"I will wait for the authorities here," Diona said.

"We can't leave you here," Amber said. "What if they come back?"

Just then, two siren-wailing blue and white Polizia boats charged past the workshop, throwing so much water against the dock, the boat moored there lifted nearly up to the workshop floor.

"Hurry," Diona said. "They're on the run. I'll be fine. You two have a treasure to collect. Do not disappoint Essa. And try not to die before you find it."

Rick hesitated. Glancing toward the open wall of the workshop and back at Diona. "Are you sure?"

She nodded. "I will not be chased away from my home. My family has lived here for six hundred years." At Rick's continued hesitance, she said, "I will stay with a friend in Padua for a week, until the Polizia confirm it is safe to return. Will that help?"

"Just stay safe. The Russian knows where you are now."

She didn't respond to that as she finished raising the delivery door. "Go. Go. Before the gunmen return. I will leave out the other entrance."

Rick hesitated still, but she shooed them both with a hand gesture. He leaned in and gave her a quick kiss on the cheek. Diona made a face as a flush of color rose in her pale cheeks.

"Trouble," she muttered. To Amber, she said, "Watch your back. Around him as well as around the people with guns."

"Thank you for everything," Amber said.

She and Rick slid out the door into a wide alley. He checked the surroundings, hunting the roofs above them as well as the canal at one end and another stone pathway at the other. No people.

And most importantly, no guns.

They took off at a jog, making their way back to the train station.

"Where to now?" she asked, a little breathless as they hurried through the labyrinth of streets and canals.

"Argentina."

TWELVE

VICTOR KNOCKED on his boss's door. The thick wood created a dull sort of echo.

He entered at a word from Mikhailov.

The study in the Rome mansion was a favorite of the boss's. Although Victor found the shrine to Mikhailov's murdered sons a little hard to bear. But the boss liked all the pictures and the little candle-covered altar in the corner of the room. The cleaning staff kept the candles lit, ensured they were regularly rotated. Even when Mikhailov wasn't in residence.

For Victor, the reminders were too terrible. Seeing his boss broken had been hard to witness. And ten years later, those memories were still fresh. The boss couldn't let them go. Neither could Victor.

"Important news, Victor?" he asked when Victor closed the door behind him.

"It's Kalashnik. His men shot up the Venetian woman's workshop."

"Did they get…what O'Neill and Ross found?"

"The Polizia arrived before they got into the workshop. Far as we can tell, Ross and O'Neill got away with whatever they found there. We covered them as they left so none of Kalashnik's people could stop them. But Kalashnik will know where they're going."

"So long as we also know."

"I already have people on the way there. Argentina."

Mikhailov stared at his desk for a long time, then his gaze moved to the picture of his sons he kept on the corner. It was a picture of them at a soccer game together. They were in their early twenties. Just starting out in life. The oldest, Petrov, had just graduated from university and was on his way to medical school. The soccer game was their celebration.

Kalashnik had them murdered a week later. Revenge for Mikhailov taking over one of Kalashnik's most lucrative gun running businesses.

"Have the jet readied," Mikhailov said, his voice quiet, his gaze still on the picture of his sons.

"Let us go and get the relic for you, boss. Kalashnik will have people there now. It could be dangerous."

Mikhailov lifted his gaze and met Victor's. The stare was distant, his boss's thoughts turned to future matters. "We leave in twenty."

"Okay."

Victor left his boss to ensure they had enough men waiting in Argentina.

And enough ammunition.

THIRTEEN

THE BUENOS AIRES AIRPORT BUSTLED, people coming and going from the arrivals lounge, noisy conversations in a variety of languages but mostly dominated by Spanish, though with an accent Amber found impossible to decipher. While her ability to read Spanish was decent, her spoken Spanish was mediocre at best. Add the Argentina accent and slang and she was lost.

Fortunately, Rick's language skills came in handy, allowing them to navigate the crowded lounge and get through passport control without their American accents waving red flags for anyone listening nearby. The guy at passport control didn't even blink at the large white man with an American passport speaking perfect Argentinian Spanish, either. Which was probably something she'd think about later since *she* wondered about Rick's perfect Argentine accent. There was a story there, she was sure.

An associate of Rick's met them near the tinted glass doors leading out to taxis and the warm, sunny midday.

"You look like shit," the man said, giving Rick a friendly,

back-pounding hug. "What treasure are you looking for this week?"

"Just a little something for a friend. Nothing big," Rick said, hitching his backpack up on his shoulder.

The man scoffed. "Nothing valuable, right? Nothing worth anything."

"Na. Just a little fun."

The man made no effort to hide his disbelief. He turned to Amber, who'd been hovering behind Rick, and smiled. "Carlos Juarez." He held his hand out for her to shake.

"Adele Winters," Amber introduced herself with one of her aliases.

She didn't think that would throw the Russian off for long. Especially since he knew who Rick was. But she hoped it would at least keep anyone who might have heard that the name Amber Ross was worth money from quickly identifying her.

On the train to Bologna, where they gone to catch the flight to Buenos Aires—hoping Mikhailov's people would check the airports closer to Venice first—she'd disappeared into a bathroom and shoved her normally pin straight brown hair up under a wig of darker brown curls. She'd also put in brown contacts to cover her blue eyes. It wasn't a huge change. Nothing that would draw attention. But the curls and darker eye color gave her face just enough of a different look, she was harder to recognize at a glance. Especially in pictures.

She'd used the Adele Winters i.d. for the flight as well. Interpole and Inspector Haviard, already knew that alias, which meant she'd have to burn it soon. But at the moment, she wasn't hiding from Inspector Haviard. She hoped it took Mikhailov and his people at least some time to link Adele Winters to Amber Ross.

Just a little more time. That was all they needed.

First, though, a car and a safe place to examine the contents of the leather packet. They hadn't dared even pull the packet out of Rick's backpack since he'd slipped it in there on the way to the Venice train station.

Rick had used one of her burner phones to call his associate here before their arrival. Helpful to have a treasure hunter with her who was used to moving around different parts of the world. Her sphere of play hadn't yet brought her to Argentina. And once again, she was sorry not to be here on a vacation.

Would Carlos know if they had good shoes here?

She gave the man a once over. He was about five foot five, wiry but with maybe a little extra around the middle, and his dark black hair was cut into one of the most magnificent mullets she'd ever seen in real life. He was clean shaven, but she couldn't guess his age. Maybe mid-thirties, mid-forties. He was dressed in a short-sleeved button-down shirt and tan pants that suited the warm, dry weather.

Hard to tell if he would know or have opinions on the best places to buy women's shoes, though. She'd just have to keep her eyes open.

Well, first she still had to survive their current ordeal. But then, if she did, she was treating herself to new shoes. Maybe more than one pair. Survival called for a reward.

"I've got a car for you," Carlos said to Rick. "This way."

The closed-top Jeep looked like something that would take them over city streets and through jungles. Although, Rick hadn't mentioned jungles. And actually, they were more likely to end up in deserts in this part of South America. Still. The green and black Jeep looked like something they could cross a desert in without it breaking down.

"Supplies are in the back. Usual fees."

"Money'll be in your account in the next hour," Rick said. They paused at the Jeep, and Rick gave Carlos a very level look. "If someone working with or for a man with a Russian accent asks about us, we weren't here."

Carlos's eyebrows rose and he let out a soft whistle. "I heard about Jacque," he said after a moment. "You need to watch your back, my friend."

"We'll be fine. Stay sharp, just in case… News travels. Friends end up in the crossfire sometimes."

"Yes. I'll be sure to steer clear of the soccer grounds today. I hear a certain individual is fond of that sport. You'd do well to avoid the area around the stadium today, too. River is playing Boca, and it will be chaos. Probably some fights. Good place to hide…activities."

Rick's mouth quirked at one corner. "Thanks for the warning." He gave Carlos a clap on the shoulder and they climbed into the Jeep.

He had them out of the airport and on the highway into Buenos Aires before he said, "Get the packet out. Let's see where we're going."

FOURTEEN

THEY DROVE the long way around the city to avoid the soccer stadium, finding parking not far from the Recoleta Cemetery. But rather than go in with the tourists, they settled themselves in a fast-food restaurant in the mall at one side of the cemetery, where they could watch tourists pass on their way toward the famous city of the dead's entrance.

"No one followed," she said, stuffing fries into her mouth. "At least not yet."

"They'll find us here sooner rather than later," Rick said. "We have to work fast. But after the cemetery is mostly empty."

"You have a way to keep us in there after closing?"

He flashed her a smug smile. Diona was right. His smile really should be illegal.

"I've got a friend," he said. "I lived down here for a few years, about a decade ago. Love the Argentinians."

"So long as they love you, and you didn't have to flee for you life or anything, we'll be fine."

Another smile.

"We gonna talk about what happened at Diona's workshop?" They hadn't discussed it on the journey here, because they'd had no real privacy. And in the Jeep, they'd been busy unpacking and deciphering the things Essa had hidden in the leather packet.

"The…" Rick glanced around. "*He* wants you dead. Seems obvious what happened."

"He wants what we're hunting for," she murmured back. "Seems smarter to let us find it, then take it from us, and then kill us, rather than killing us before it's retrieved. Why try to kill us at the workshop?"

"Probably thought they could get the map before we did and the rest would be easy. I doubt *he* wants us to actually get our hands on the relic."

"Why not?"

Rick let out a long breath. "Promise not to get upset."

"Too late. Your murder has now just gotten more painful."

"After I've saved your life, though, right?"

"Of course. Continue."

"So, I told you the device isn't just a machine for measuring the pulse rate."

"You mentioned that, yes." And then never explained because Inspector Haviard showed up.

"What it's supposed to really do is…very dangerous."

He'd said that, too, without going into detail. She waited for those details now. When he didn't provide them, she sipped her soda through a straw noisily because it annoyed him. If he didn't explain, and soon, he was definitely going to die in a much more brutal way than her original murder plans had called for.

He glanced around the restaurant. While there were a lot of Spanish speaking locals, because of the type of fast food this place served, there were an awful lot of tourists, too. Speaking all kinds of languages. Including English. Which meant they could be overheard.

He scooted around the little round metal table to sit in a chair next to her, where he could still keep an eye on the people outside the large front windows.

"The reason Essa hid it, rather than bringing it back to Italy… It's the same reason Galileo never claimed priority for creating the machine. His pulse measurement machine was built while he was in Padua, when his workshop produced machines suitable for warfare."

"Like the calculator?" Galileo invented a type of calculator good for quickly figuring out things like distance and height to targets. "He didn't hesitate to not only take credit for that, but to defend his priority in inventing it."

"A minor contribution to battlefield logistics. Compared to the pulse machine."

"The thing I created for the…for him, was done with all available data and details. And all it could have possibly done was measure a pulse rate with some degree of accuracy. What else could something like that do?"

She'd built the thing. Reproduced it from every record she could find. What she'd developed could not have done anything that would be cause for all this secrecy.

And maybe that's how the Russian figured out it was a forgery. Maybe he knew whatever it was Rick was trying so very hard not to tell her. And when the machine Jacque sold Mikhailov couldn't do whatever this was, he'd realized it was a fake.

She let out a slow breath. "How he knew?"

"Probably how he knew," Rick confirmed without having to ask what she meant. "You can murder me later."

"Adding to the weapons I'll use as we speak. What does the machine really do?"

"Turns out, instead of measuring the pulse—which is what he told Viviani it did—what he'd actually built was a way to stop someone's heart."

"Huh?" She frowned as she considered that. It didn't seem possible given the technology of the time. "How?"

"I don't really understand how it works," Rick admitted. "I

only know what Bertolo told me that Essa told him. She refused to discuss it in detail. But…according to her, the Nazi colonel who'd found and kept the machine…used it. Experimented. On concentration camp prisoners." Rick lowered his voice further. "He kept records."

"Ew." That was pretty horrible, on all levels. And she was certain any further details would enrage her, and haunt her nightmares, so she didn't ask for an explanation of those experiments. Instead, she asked, "What happened to those records?"

"Essa used some of the documents they found to ensure the colonel was convicted of war crimes and hanged. The ones that had to do with the pulse rate machine, she hid with the machine. She swore to the end of her life the documents and the machine were too dangerous to reveal to the public." He shrugged. "I only know as much as she told Bertolo, and he was certain she hadn't told him everything. But given how much the Russian wants to add the machine to his collection, and the fact that he knew we'd sold him a fake, I'd say he's heard some of the same legends about that relic, and it's part of the reason he wants it."

"Part of the reason?"

Rick held her gaze but didn't comment.

Implying the Russian maybe wanted to *use* the machine. "But… Why would he need a machine that stops someone's heart when he obviously has no problem killing people with more conventional weapons. He can just have people shot. With lots of bullets. Exactly the way they tried to kill us."

"Those kinds of murders look like murder. Maybe he wants to kill people in a way that can't look like murder? How do I know? I'm not a murderer."

"But…there's poison. There's radiation. There's accidents. There's all kinds of ways to kill people." She made a face. "That's an unpleasant thought. Anyway, stopping someone's heart? What good is that to him? Specifically? So much so, he spent a fortune and went through Jacque for the relic."

"Best I can figure, it's a way to avoid a murder looking like a murder, in a way that can't be traced with forensics. Someone's heart stops, no one is going to stand up and say the Russian must have murdered them using a seventeenth century machine invented by Galileo that no one thinks exists."

Right. Forensics. Forensics picked up poison. Radiation. The obvious fact of a body riddled with bullets.

But that had never stopped Mikhailov from having people killed. Jacque for one. Everyone knew he'd been responsible for Jacque's murder. Yet Interpol tracked down her and Rick. They hadn't arrested Mikhailov. Getting away with murder was like… his job. It's what he did.

"Who the hell would he want to kill so badly, and yet not get caught doing it, that he'd look to a maybe-not-even-real device like this?"

Rick raised his brows. "That's the question, isn't it? Who's he after, who's he want dead this much, but can't actually afford to have it look like the person was murdered?"

"A country leader? Someone with even more power?" That thought was terrifying.

"If he doesn't shoot us first, maybe we can ask him."

She silently sipped on her soda as the implications sunk in. "Rick," she said slowly. "We can't let him have the real relic. We can't. Whoever he wants dead… Just. We can't."

"I wasn't ever going to give him the real relic," Rick said. "I was going to use it to bargain for your life. But I don't want him to have the real thing any more than you do."

"We can't give him another fake. He'll just keep coming for us." She set her paper cup down, slowly. "How do we get out of this, without letting him have the relic?"

Rick didn't answer.

Which was exactly the answer she'd been afraid of.

FIFTEEN

MIKHAILOV HUNG up the phone and snubbed his cigar out in the ashtray on the corner of the small desk in his Argentinian suite. He stared for a long moment at the desk in front of him, his expression hard, his dark eyes glittering.

Victor stood at attention to one side of the desk, carefully keeping his expression neutral. Overhearing some of his boss's conversations came with the job. Ignoring what was said during those conversations was a necessary survival skill. One he and Nikko had learned well over the years.

When Mikhailov finally spoke, his voice was tight. "I must have the pulse rate machine. There can be no more delays."

"They're at the cemetery," Nikko said. "Looking for another clue?"

"No. Essa Martolli found the relic here. She left it here. They will retrieve it from the cemetery. And we will retrieve it from them." He looked up.

Victor carefully didn't react to the look in his boss's eyes. He knew that look. That look meant someone was going to die. Soon.

"Kalashnik's position in the government has been confirmed," Mikhailov said slowly. "He is almost untouchable now."

"Then it's too late?" Nikko said.

Mikhailov gave him a look, and Nikko straightened his shoulders.

"No, my Nikko. It is not too late. He still desires the relic. Or he would not have sent his people after Ross and O'Neill. He would not be trying to steal it before I can get it. He's revealed himself. There is still time."

"You sure he'll accept it, knowing it's coming from you?" Nikko asked.

"He'll accept it. He won't be able to resist."

Mikhailov considered them both. Victor kept his chin high and his gaze on the wall across from the desk, well used to his boss's scrutiny.

"His people here," Mikhailov said after a moment, "they will die alongside the art forger. It will look like O'Neill and Ross killed them."

Victor nodded. These were the sorts of orders that happened without actual words, and he'd become very adept at understanding his boss's orders without Mikhailov having to spell them out.

"He won't be there," Nikko's said.

"Of course not. He would never leave his stronghold. But it will not protect him." The boss smiled.

Victor glanced at the desk so he didn't have to see the expression. Years of pain and anger and blood lust lived in that dark smile. Rage so deep there was no bottom. Victor understood those feelings. Well. But it was difficult to look at.

"He made a terrible enemy when he killed my sons," Mikhailov said quietly. "And he knows it. But he thinks I have accepted there is nothing I can do to him. He is wrong. He is not quite untouchable yet. But…" He waited for both Victor and Nikko to meet his gaze. "We must have the relic."

"It's yours, boss," Nikko said.

Victor gave a brief nod. "We won't let you down."

"I know you won't," the boss said. "I know you won't."

SIXTEEN

AS THE SUN started to go down, the tourist crowds thinned and shadows fell across the cemetery's red brick wall. Amber and Rick left the mall and made their way through the decorative garden and souvenir vendor carts to the main entrance to Recoleta, where white columns and white brick caught the glittering sunset light, turning the stones pink.

When Amber headed for the main gate, Rick took her arm and walked her to a side desk. In his Argentinean Spanish, he asked for someone.

"Friend?" she murmured to him.

"Friend."

A few moments passed. Then a woman from a side office door emerged. She greeted Rick with a warm smile and kisses on both cheeks. Which Amber dutifully ignored. And wasn't irritated by. Not even a little bit.

"I am surprised to see you," the woman said in English, her accent making the words curl into a purr. She glanced at Amber briefly before returning her full focus on Rick. She said something to him in Spanish.

Rick answered in English. "We'll need to stay well after closing. Please."

The woman pulled in a deep breath. She was a pretty, petit woman, maybe five foot two, and slim but curvy in her dark blue uniform with the cemetery's crest on the front of the shirt. Her blond hair was swept up on top of her head in a neat bun, and her dark eyes narrowed a little every time she glanced at Amber.

"I appreciate this, Yadira," Rick said. "I wouldn't ask if it weren't important."

Yadira pursed her lips, an expression that somehow made her mouth look lush instead of pinched. How did she do that? Makeup? Really good lip-liner? Amber would have asked if the cemetery guard hadn't continued to throw her strangely narrow-eyed looks.

Yadira said something else to Rick in Spanish, then waved him to follow. She let them into the cemetery through a side gate marked with an official looking sign Amber translated as Employee's Only.

Rick thanked Yadira again as they past into the cemetery grounds. She waved him away, smiling slyly as she said one last thing before closing the door.

"So... Yadira wants to cook you a steak? Did I translate that right?"

"Steak in Argentina is beautiful. We get time, you should try it."

"I'll consider that if we survive the night."

"Yeah." He let out a long breath. "Big if there."

"Don't remind me."

They slipped through the mausoleums at the front of the cemetery and down a side alley, moving deeper into the city of the dead.

The Recoleta Cemetery did resemble a walled city within the city. The ancient tombs and mausoleums lined stone paths like houses along a road. Small trees and little squares decorated the intersections of those "streets." There were even road signs and a map to navigate the complex grounds. Some tombs were elaborate, huge, and well maintained. Others were sparse and simple. Some rows contained identical tombs, while along other paths each tomb was more elaborate than the next.

Under different circumstances, Amber would have liked a proper tour of the place, stopping to hear stories about all the famous mausoleums, with their famous—and infamous—occupants.

But as the sun set, and the cemetery grew dark, she couldn't quite dispel the idea that they were being watched. That something wandered this cemetery. And that if they weren't careful, whatever the something was, it would find them before they could get out.

She shivered.

Rick frowned at her. "You cold?"

"Nope. Creeped out walking around a cemetery in the dark."

He handed her a flashlight she hadn't noticed him carrying. "If I let you control the light will that help?"

"Yes. But also, if there are zombies or vampires or anything else in here that want to eat us, I can run faster than you. You know that, right?"

"Don't worry. I brought the good cross and holy water."

She frowned. "That was a joke, right? Right?"

He smiled at her over his shoulder, but didn't answer.

They'd moved well past the main entrance and off the more beaten tourist path before Rick finally pulled the leather packet out of his backpack. Amber had carefully refolded the map on its yellowing paper and replaced it to keep it safe and hidden. Besides the map, there was also an old-fashioned metal key in the packet. And that had been its entire contents. If then needed anything else to retrieve the relic, it hadn't been in the packet Essa had left in Venice.

For all the secrecy around, and difficulty in retrieving, the map, the map itself wasn't all that complicated. It gave a brief sketch of the cemetery, a path through the city of tombs to a specific row, showed squares representing the mausoleums along that row, and marked the appropriate grave with a red dot.

There weren't any inscriptions. No names to identify the correct tomb. They'd have to count and hope they got the right one, that the map was still accurate after all these years.

And that no one had found the pulse rate machine during those intervening years and taken it home. Or destroyed it.

As they worked their way through the tombs, Amber worked hard not to consider that last option.

SEVENTEEN

THE DARKNESS SETTLED SLOWLY around them. A gray twilight that seemed to eat light and made seeing even more difficult than full darkness. Lights along the high walls circling the cemetery lit up, but they were all pointing outward. Not much air moved through the cemetery, but occasionally a breeze ruffled the tree leaves, casting flickering shadows across the stones paths.

They followed the map as best they could, whispering when they had to talk, and trying not to make too much noise. She wasn't sure why Rick was being quiet. For her part, she didn't want to wake up any scary things that might be sleeping in here.

A black flash streaked across the paving stones in front of them, right through the flashlight's beam of light. Amber gasped.

"Just a cat," Rick said. "They're all over here. This is as much their city as it is the dead's."

"Cats and dead people. Good. Good. Sounds like a real party." She gripped the flashlight harder when her hand started to tremble.

"For someone who deals with so many of the dead's relics

and artifacts, you're pretty squeamish about a few cats and corpses."

"Yeah, well, there's a reason I specialize in technological inventions and not reliquaries. I'm not a bone person."

"There's an off-color joke in there, but I'm afraid you'll hit me with the flashlight if I make it."

"I will. Already considering it. Even without the joke."

"But then who will protect you from the mummies and zombies and vampires?"

"Who said anything about mummies? I never mentioned mummies. Are you telling me there are mummies in here?"

Rick's chuckle did not make her feel any better.

They passed a giant angel statue, holding a lamp high in one hand, her wings spearing into the sky, a look of benign tolerance on her face as she gazed at the path. Three dark cats, their eyes glittering in the ambient light from the surrounding city, sat at the base of the statue and gazed back up at the angel. None of them looked at Amber and Rick as they passed.

She shivered again. Cats were scary.

They reached the path they needed, near the back of the cemetery, as far from the entrance as was possible. The row of gray stone and black marble tombs were one path away from the back wall, in a section not well traveled based on the weeds and overgrowth. No famous tombs here. Just ordinary citizens. Well, probably wealthy still to have been buried here. But probably without relatives around anymore to look after the tombs.

The mausoleum embellishments were lean here, too. A few stone planters outside the doors. Some scrollwork in the marble maybe. But mostly just squat, stone structures, with little peaked roofs, and metal doors or gates obscuring the burial beds beyond. Some were small enough they probably didn't have very many buried in them or only contained urns, while others were large enough she might be able to stand her full height inside. None were as large as some of the more elaborate tombs in other parts of the cemetery.

A relatively ordinary row of houses for the dead, in a back suburb of the dead's city.

Quietly, without looking at the map he held, Rick walked along the row. Amber counted the tombs in her head as they moved toward the spot that had been marked on Essa's map.

One mausoleum they passed had a broken door, revealing an interior so pitch black, it was impossible to see inside. Thankfully! As the night got darker and cooler, her desire to see corpses diminished considerably.

Instead of the generally faint smell of drying flowers and living trees, the occasional overwhelming whiff of roses, this close to the wall some of the city crept in, a little punch of garlic in the background from some nearby restaurant.

That reminder that there was a city just beyond the red brick perimeter wall, that there were living people still out there somewhere, that if she looked up, she'd see lights in windows on the nearby high-rise buildings, kept her from running screaming into the night.

Still, she had to clamp her lips together to keep from screeching when a cat zipped past just behind her.

At Rick's raised brows, she snarled and mouthed, "Cats!" And then wasn't sure why she wasn't talking out loud. Like the cats might overhear and attack?

She rolled her eyes at herself and concentrated on where she was in her count. There. A black marble tomb, sitting between another black marble mausoleum and a pale stone structure. Nothing about it stood out. It was one of the larger ones, tall enough for her to stand up inside, but probably not tall enough for Rick. Maybe six or seven feet wide. A single stair up to the dark, weathered metal door with no additional gate in front of it. The name Ezekiel was embossed on the door, but no other markers. No dates. No other names.

Nothing that stood out. Nothing that marked it as unique.

She exchanged a look with Rick, then stepped closer to the door. A gentle tug confirmed it was locked. Whether that meant it had remained locked after all this time or not… Well, they'd find out.

If the key that had been inside the leather packet opened the tomb, the lock was the same, and likely no one had been in here for decades. If the key didn't work, the lock had been changed.

And they were fucked.

A scrabbling noise behind them swung Amber around. Another cat darted past, a blur of motion hard to see in the darkness. She swung the flashlight around. More eyes glittered in the deep shadows, blinked, and vanished into the surroundings.

"How many cats are in here?" she asked, scanning the crypts with her meager flashlight beam.

"Lots. Why? Not a cat person?"

"Never minded them before. But honestly, more of a dog person."

"Why didn't I know this about you?"

"Never came up. Never been surrounded by a cat army before."

"Huh. Would have pegged you for a cat person."

"Why? Because I'm fussy about shoes, right? It's the fussiness." Her breathing was coming too fast. She'd hyperventilate soon if she didn't calm down. The weird cat-dog conversation wasn't helping.

The hairs on her neck rose and a shiver crawled down her spine. She was certain someone was watching them.

More glittering eyes winking past in the flashlight beam. So many cats. Or just a few that kept moving around?

Rick produced the key for the tomb. He'd moved it from the leather pouch to his pants pocket before they'd left the fast-food restaurant. He held it up. They both considered the three inch long, heavy, old-fashioned metal key, with a four-prong bit at the end. Then they considered the small keyhole on the tomb door where that metal key was supposed to fit.

"It'll fit," Rick said, his voice low.

"It'll fit," she said.

Nerves and worries tightened her gut as Rick slipped the key into the lock. It slid in with a little wiggle. He took a deep breath. She held hers.

He turned the key.

A griding noise that made her wince. A little grunt from Rick as he used two hands to keep the key moving.

Then a click.

The nerves in her stomach started dancing. With excitement now.

Rick tugged the door and it swung outward.

EIGHTEEN

THE INSIDE of the small mausoleum was pitch black, impossible to see into. Amber held the light beam pointing down at the stone stair at the base of the door. Her pulse pounded so hard it almost hurt. A mix of excitement and fear gripping her. Sweat trickled down her spine, despite the cool night air. Suddenly, her backpack felt itchy and uncomfortable.

Rick leaned into the doorway, then turned back to her. "Flashlight?"

She nodded. But didn't move the light up.

A weird, dry, musty smell emanated from the open tomb. Not rot. Nothing quite so gag-inducing. But it was still that dank smell of thing no longer living.

"Why did Essa have to hide this here?" she whispered. "Couldn't have found a nice hole in the jungle to bury it in?"

"You in a jungle?" Rick asked, his brows raised. "That would ruin your shoes."

"Better than me inside a mausoleum."

"I still can't get over the woman who loves old things doesn't like wandering around crypts."

"I love fixing and restoring old things. Can't fix and restore a dead body."

"Unless you're Dr. Frankenstein."

"Which I am not. I never got my Ph.D."

"Want me to go in alone?"

"And leave me out here with the scary cats? No. I'm going in. Just… Gearing myself up for it."

"Shine the light inside. If you can see what you're walking into, you might feel better about it."

"Or I'll freak out and go running to the scary cats for protection." She pulled in a breath. "Either way." She lifted the flashlight.

Inside the crypt, on either side, were three stone beds, stacked one on top of the other. Each bed held a wrapped body, the material covering them gray and worn with time. No bones stuck out from the shrouds. No way to confirm an actual corpse lay under them. If she was very careful about where she looked, she could pretend she wasn't desecrating an actual tomb.

Murmuring an apology to the dead for disturbing their sleep —and hoping that kept them asleep—she followed Rick inside.

He went right to the back of the crypt, which was longer than it was wide.

Walking between the corpses was not the easiest thing she'd ever done. She didn't want to touch anything, so she sucked in her shoulders as if that would help.

The flashlight wavered against the far wall, over Rick's back. He hunted the stones, pressing against various sections of the marble.

"You think she put it in a cubbyhole or something?" Amber whispered.

"Where else? She wouldn't have wanted to leave it out in the open."

That made sense. But since they hadn't brought a crowbar, she wasn't sure how they were going to get into any of the cubbyholes at the back of the crypt. And assuming some of those cubbies had urns or bones in them, she'd prefer not to go breaking into them anyway.

"I'd have made a terrible grave robber," she muttered.

"Too honest?"

"Ha! Too squeamish."

"This is why I don't take you on my treasure hunts."

"I thought that was because you didn't want me to kill you when you got my shoes ruined."

"That too." He pressed a few more spots on the wall.

She held the flashlight pointed so it would illuminate what he was doing, but she kept glancing back at the beds, and the corpses laying on them. If one of those moved, she was going to scream.

Something in the shadows did seem to move. She pressed her lips together so she didn't make any ridiculous sounds. Then leaned toward the dancing shadow when she realized the only reason it was "dancing" was because her hand was shaking and making the flashlight beam jump around.

The darker patch of shadow stretched from behind the corpse on the middle bunk to her right. For a brief moment, she had the horrifying thought that it was a cat, sleeping with the corpse, and that cat was going to tear into them for disturbing its sleep. Then she remembered that there'd been no way for a cat to get in here ahead of them, and it would have been dead had it been caught in here the last time the tomb was opened.

That just got her to thinking about armies of dead cats marching around the cemetery.

"I need the light for a second," she said, warning Rick before turning it away from the back wall.

"I'm not having any luck anyway," he said. "What did you find?"

She swung the flashlight around to point it at the middle bed, illuminating the gray shroud-covered body. Wanting to close her eyes, but afraid if she did the corpse would definitely move, she squatted down to better see to the back of the bed.

And there, her flashlight reflected off a large, brown wooden box.

That looked, on the outside, so very close to the replica she'd created.

She pressed a hand to her mouth. "Is that the—"

"Pulse rate machine? Looks like it."

"It's—"

"Just like you built it."

"I can't believe we've—"

"Found it." Rick let out a long breath. "Me neither."

"And now," said a voice from the open crypt door, "I will take it."

NINETEEN

AMBER STOOD SO FAST, she nearly slammed into the stone crypt beds. She swung the flashlight around, shining it into the face of a man blocking the doorway as Rick stepped between her and the man. The man in the doorway held a gun pointed at them. But he had raised his other hand against the light.

"I'll shoot before you can rush me," he said, his tone dispassionate.

Well, rushing him while he was blinded by her flashlight probably would have been a good idea. If she'd thought about it. Which she hadn't.

She lowered the light just enough that it no longer shone directly in his eyes. She was a little afraid he'd shoot randomly if she didn't.

He blinked a few times. Then looked around the crypt. His gun never moved. Never wavered. Never shook.

It took her several moments to realize she'd seen the man before. At the Met. One of the two men who'd been walking through the museum with guns tucked under their suit jackets.

He was a big man with wide shoulders inside his well-tailored, dark suit. The shoulder holster beneath the jacket didn't disturb the lines much, which was impressive. He had a thick jaw, clean shaven around a small goatee, and his dark hair was cut tight to his head. Small, dark eyes that were impossible to read. And an expression that could have cracked granite.

So probably not someone they could negotiate with.

"I'm sure we can talk about this," Rick said. Obviously not seeing the same thing she was seeing in that man's face.

"Boss wants what he wants. I'll take it now."

"Do you even know what it is?" Amber asked, stalling because they had to get past this guy if they were going to survive.

She'd rather not lose the relic to him either, but first they had to survive.

"Doesn't matter what it is. Boss wants it." He shrugged. "But I know what it is."

"So you know it's more than just a…collectible, right?" she asked, wondering how much Mikhailov actually knew. Not that his man might know everything, but… Stalling.

Just behind him, another man came into view and whispered something to him. The second large man from the museum. He was a bit younger, with a lot more hair on his head and a lot less on his face. His suit was as immaculate as the first man's.

Such good fashion sense. Shame they were the bad guys.

When the two men stopped talking, the one with the gun in the doorway said, "Pick up the relic."

Amber swallowed hard. Picking up the relic. That involved getting it from behind a corpse. She didn't want to do that. She wanted to make Rick do that. This was all his fault anyway.

Rick nodded and gave her back a little rub before shifting positions with her so he could better reach the wooden box.

Amber kept her attention on the man with the gun and tried hard not to think about the fact that Rick was leaning over a corpse. Probably touching a corpse. She would not think about that.

She felt him straighten behind her and finally turned a little to look at him.

Her breath caught again, to see Galileo's actual pulse rate machine. Right there. A thing so many thought was just a made up story. Looking so close to the one she'd recreated from just… diary entries and letters and hundreds-year-old innuendo and gossip. She'd worked with such scant information. Yet…at least from the outside, the box holding the pieces of the device looked so similar.

She'd gotten some of the details wrong, of course. How could she not? This one had leather straps around the entire box with little nails tacking them over the structure. Hers had only had leather straps over the lid. The clip holding the lid in place on this one was less elaborate than the one she'd used, too. But the size was right, roughly two feet wide by one tall. In the dark it was impossible to tell, but she thought she might have also gotten the coloration and staining right on her replica.

Inside, there should be a pendulum on a long, knotted cord, wrapped around a hand crank for lowering the pendulum. There should be an iron disk at the base of the box, for the pendulum to swing over, with astrology symbols circling it. She'd never learned why the iron disk was necessarily decorative, but at the time Galileo invented this, he was still doing the occasional astrological chart and hadn't dismissed astrology as a science yet. So she'd assumed it was symbolic.

There should also be a folded ruler which could be unfolded and set into the center of the iron disk. The place where the pendulum synched with a patients pulse along the ruler was supposed to mark the heart rate.

At least, that's how it worked in the other, later created device from Santorio. With Santorio's invention, the skill of the doctor using it was as important as the device itself. Galileo's supposedly relied less on the ability of the doctor to properly use the machine. But no one knew how.

And now that she knew the machine didn't just measure pulse rates, but supposedly stopped the actual heart from pumping… There had to be more in the box than what she'd designed and recreated.

The man blocking the doorway waved his gun at them. "Let's go. Bring it outside. We don't have much time."

"We should check inside," Amber said, still stalling but also insanely curious. What was different about this one compared to her reproduction? What was really inside that box? What had she missed? What had been left out of all the writings?

What had Galileo really created?

Amber glanced hopefully at the man with the gun. She didn't want to die, but she'd hate dying even more if she didn't get her curiosity satisfied first. "You don't want to risk another fake, right?" she said. "We should check."

The second man moved up closer to the first again, but his back was to the tomb as he scanned the surroundings. The man in the crypt doorway stared for a long moment at the box. Then he leaned back to murmur something with his associate.

Amber couldn't hear much. Something about other men? There must be more of them out there. Running away seemed less and less viable an option. Not that they could run with that big gun pointed at them. Still, a very large part of her body and instincts was insisting that running away was exactly what she should be doing at that moment.

The adrenaline rushing through her body made her jumpy, and it took monumental effort not to do something stupid that would get her shot. Knowing there were more people out there somewhere, probably all with guns, was a good deterrent to her adrenaline-fueled bad ideas.

The first man straightened away from his compatriot and said, "We only have a minute. Others will be here soon. Open the box. But we don't have time to go through it."

Amber faced Rick, held his gaze a moment, then opened the box.

Her breath caught. So so close!

She'd missed details here, too, of course. The pendulum was a brighter brass color than she'd expected. She'd aged hers to look older. Just as she'd aged the iron disk, and the real one looked more well-preserved than her version. She'd gotten the symbols right—Galileo had used a standard astrological disk—but there were crystals and stones set into the real disk that had never been mentioned anywhere. The folding ruler was where she'd placed it in her version, against one side of the box. She'd also gotten the shape of the pendulum right, a cylinder weight with a sharp point at one end. But where she'd used a knotted rope made of blue twisted cloth, the pendulum chain in the real relic was formed from brass links and the links for aligning to the right length for the pendulum swing were marked with darkened metal. The chain also had a large, thick circle of metal, like an oversized ring, at the top, which was another detail she'd missed.

But even with all that, she'd managed to get so close she could barely believe it.

She wanted desperately to study the thing more. To learn how it worked. How on earth something like this could stop a heart. But as she reached out to touch the pendulum, Rick snapped the lid on the box down.

She glared at him. He'd almost clipped her fingers.

He gave her a little head shake.

Okay. She wasn't supposed to even touch the thing?

"It's authentic," Rick said.

The man in the doorway waved his gun again, motioning them out of the tomb.

Amber started forward.

And stepped on something soft and squishy.

That something screeched. Amber screeched. Guy with the

gun shouted. Amber fell backward into Rick. Rick fell against one of the crypt beds.

And the box in his hands started to tumble.

Everyone lurched for it. Amber caught it moments before Rick's hands also wrapped around it again.

Her heart pounded so hard she thought she might actually pass out before they were shot. She made a face at Rick. He blew out a relieved breath.

The man in the doorway straightened his suit jacket with a one-handed snap. "What the hell was that?"

Amber looked around. Yellow eyes blinked at them from the back of the tomb. She nearly dropped the box and lurched backward again. Until she realized it was another one of the damned cats.

"Cat. What the hell is it doing inside the crypt?"

"Must have come in while we were searching," Rick murmured.

"Picked a stupid place for a nap." She shivered. Stepping on something soft and squishy inside a burial chamber was a sensory experience she could have done without.

The man in the doorway cleared his throat. "Are we done playing with the animals?"

She scowled at him, but since he was still holding a gun on her, she kept her opinion of that sarcastic comment to herself. For now.

"Out." He motioned with his gun again. "The boss wants to see this for himself."

From behind the man with the gun, where Amber couldn't see, a voice said, "Yes, Ms. Ross. I very much want to see the *real* relic this time. We will see exactly how good your forgery was."

TWENTY

AMBER SWALLOWED HARD. That voice. The accent. Oh, this couldn't be good. She looked back at Rick, still holding the relic, the darkness of the tomb shrouding them in an illusion of security. Security they were about the shatter walking out of this crypt.

Rick closed his eyes briefly before meeting her gaze.

"Russian?" she mouthed.

"The Russian," he mouthed back.

"Here?"

Her heart thudded so hard now she was starting to see spots at the edge of her vision. A part of her had thought she and Rick would be able to talk themselves out of this mess when they were just dealing with Mikhailov's men. But with the Russian himself here, standing just outside the crypt, waiting to see the real relic, her hopes for survival had just plummeted.

The man in the doorway waved his gun at her again, gesturing them out of the tomb.

Sweat coated her back, and she could smell her own panic. Her brain ran away to hide in a corner, so she couldn't even begin to think of an escape plan. Rick, stilling holding the relic in both hands, tapped her back gently with his shoulder. The contact helped.

A little.

This time, as she moved forward, she watched the ground and gunman at the same time. Mikhailov probably wouldn't tolerate another cat mishap. And the dual attention meant she didn't step on any more cats.

Unfortunately, without that excuse, they stepped out into the open way too quickly.

The man standing in the middle of the stone path between the rows of mausoleums was exactly what she would have expected from a man nicknamed simply "the Russian." He was tall, probably six two or three, wide shoulders, and narrow hips. Older, though in the darkness his age was hard to pinpoint. His short pale hair shown like silver. His black suit was, like his men's, tailored exquisitely. And his black shoes shined in the ambient city light.

A curl of smoke rose from the cigar in his hand. The pungent scent of tobacco overwhelmed the musty scent of death and dryness, as well as the faint hint of garlic from the restaurant just the other side of the perimeter wall.

In fact, in that moment, all Amber seemed to be able to smell was that cigar. For some reason, that cigar smell felt like a threat.

Probably because a man who wanted them dead was smoking it.

There were at least six other men surrounding him, including the man who'd spoken to the one blocking the crypt doorway earlier. The Russian himself didn't hold a gun, but every other man around him did. They were arrayed in a way that two of them and the one who'd been blocking the crypt doorway watched Amber and Rick. The rest had their gazes on the surrounding cemetery.

Mikhailov removed his cigar from his mouth and said, "Amber Ross. I've looked forward to this meeting."

She, on the other hand, had not. She didn't say that out loud.

"Your skills are impressive. Had they not been used against me I might even have hired you."

She still didn't comment because telling the man about to kill you that you would never have worked for him seemed like a good way to get dead faster.

"Unfortunately, you did use your skills to thwart a plan I've been working on for many years. Delaying me when I could not afford the delay."

"Sorry?" But only because she'd pissed him off. She wasn't sure delaying his plans for the relic was such a bad thing.

"Now that you've brought me the true relic," he said, considering the tip of his cigar, "I think it's important we make sure it works." He met her gaze. "Don't you?"

"No. No. I think keeping it sealed in this box and setting it behind a glass display case seems like a better idea."

His dark eyes narrowed. Oops. Wrong thing to say.

He nodded and the man who'd blocked the tomb entrance grabbed Amber's arms.

She struggled and thrashed against the hold, instinctively, without a lot of thought behind the struggle. She might as well have been in vice clamps, though. Rick cursed and reached for her with one hand while he still clutched the box.

Another nod from Mikhailov, and one of the men standing next to him moved toward Rick.

Rick looked around like he wanted to run.

Then, to her horror, he lifted the box up over his head.

"Stop! You get closer, I'll smash this thing into a million pieces. Even Amber won't be able to fix it when I get done with it."

"Shoot him and take the box," Mikhailov said. "I want to make sure it works as it's supposed to."

Rick moved the box in a way that it sort of blocked him from the gun now pointing at him. "Shoot me, shoot the box. Destroy what you're after."

His man hesitated and glanced back at Mikhailov. The man holding Amber didn't move and didn't react even a little to her wiggling and struggling and pushing against his grip.

Which was embarrassing. She hadn't considered herself that weak. Not until just this moment.

Mikhailov stared at Rick. "You're only delaying the inevitable," he said. "And if you hand over the box now, I'll kill you quickly. If you damage it. I'll kill both of you so slowly, you'll beg to die."

Amber whimpered. She'd heard stories of the way the Russian killed people slowly. It was not good.

She didn't want to see the relic destroyed. She didn't want to be the test subject to see if it could really stop hearts. And she didn't want either her or Rick to die. By bullets or any other way.

But she had no idea how to get out of this mess.

Behind the Russian, a flurry of a half dozen cats scurried across the pathway.

"Too many cats in this place," the man holding Amber said.

"Agree," she murmured. Her brain was exploding with fear, and adrenaline raced through her blood stream. She was going to pass out if she wasn't careful.

The man coming for the relic moved toward Rick again. Rick raised the box enough to make his threat clear. The man hesitated again.

And then a man Amber hadn't seen earlier detached from the shadows of a nearby crypt, his gun raised.

The sound of gunfire shattered the quiet night.

TWENTY-ONE

THE MINUTE BULLETS started flying across the stone pathway between tombs, the man holding Amber released her.

She immediately scurried, head down, hands covering her head, toward the tomb. Her only thought was to reach cover from the bullets that were suddenly everywhere.

Rick scrambled toward the tomb right behind her. "Move, move!"

She was moving. She was moving!

They dove into the darkness. Amber bumped against the stone beds in her rush. She jerked her hands way from the wrapped body she'd almost touched.

The guy who'd held her leapt through the doorway. She and Rick spun to face him, but his attention was on the shooting outside. Using the doorway for cover, he fired out into the melee, not even glancing back at them.

The sound inside the crypt was almost as ear shatteringly loud as the sounds of bullets ricocheting off metal in Diona's workshop had been.

"Who are they?" she asked, keeping her head low.

"Kalashnik's men," the guy with the gun said.

"Who?"

"Mikhailov's rival," Rick answered since the guy with the gun was occupied shooting at people.

Who were shooting back.

"Old enemies." Rick said, talking near her ear to be heard over the racket. "Kalashnik had Mikhailov's sons assassinated."

"Ah. That's not good."

"Nope."

"Mikhailov is out there somewhere—"

"In the middle of all the flying bullets. Yep."

"Supposed Kalashnik is?"

"Possible."

"So, all bad guys all the time?"

"'Fraid so."

"And no good guys—"

"To the rescue? Nope."

"Then we're—"

"Fucked? Yes."

"Lovely. At least we have some cover."

Rick glanced around as he hitched the relic box higher in his arms. "But no way out."

The man blocking the doorway grunted and rolled backward a little into the crypt, taking cover. Blood bloomed around a wound in his shoulder.

Rick grabbed her arm one handed, while still juggling the relic, and urged her farther back into the tomb, to the rear wall, using the crypt beds as additional cover.

A cat, sitting on the chest of the corpse on the top bed, hissed at them.

Probably the same cat she'd stepped on. She snarled back at the cat.

Rick ignored them both.

"I'm not sure this is a better place to be," she said. "We're really trapped now."

"Better than getting shot."

"True."

The guy blocking the exit spun around the edge of the crypt door again and fired more into the chaos.

"Do I want to know what's happening out there and how many people are involved?" she asked.

"Probably not."

"Don't suppose this crypt—"

"Has a back exit? Not likely."

The cat hissed again and leapt off the corpse's chest, landing next to Amber. She screeched again, because why the hell was the cat jumping at her?! She hadn't stepped on it on purpose.

The cat swished its tail, the hair along its back raised. It was mostly black, with just a few patches of white around its nose, on one paw, and on the tip of its tail. The coloration made it almost impossible to see in the darkness at the back of the tomb. Except for the glittering yellow of its eyes and the occasional flash of white.

Amber made a face at the cat. The cat ignored her.

More gun fire from outside. Shouting now. Lots of shouting and cursing.

"Nikko!" the man in the doorway yelled.

And then he was out from behind the cover of the doorway, moving into the middle of the gunfight.

Which left the doorway wide open. For them to get out. But also for the people with guns to get in.

"If we go that way, we walk right into bullets," Rick said against her ear, without her even having to make the suggestions.

"We could wait until they stop shooting and hope the winner doesn't shoot us?"

"Good way to get shot," Rick said.

Yeah, she kind of thought so, too.

The cat flicked its tail at them again, then walked underneath the lower crypt bed, presumable to find a quieter place to nap.

A cool breeze filtered from the direction the cat went, making the already cold crypt feel even more ominously icy.

Frowning, she flattened herself to the stone floor as best she could while squishing into a space too small for both her and Rick.

"Son of a bitch," she muttered.

"What?" Rick leaned over her shoulder.

"There's a missing block. A whole ass missing block. Cats could wander in and out of here even with the door locked."

"Only big enough for a cat?"

She glanced up at him, smiling. "And for two determined humans."

He lifted the box. "What about this?"

"If we can squeeze out, it'll squeeze out."

"You first. You're smaller."

"Ah. Thank you."

She flatted under the crypt bed, sliding head first to the hole. She pushed her backpack out first, then followed. The gap was just tall and wide enough for her to wiggle out, going head first and pushing off the outside of the crypt to get her legs through. Awkward, and she accumulated a few additional scrapes and bruises, but manageable. Though she lost a tennis shoe in the process, which Rick pushed out the hole to her.

She replaced her shoe while scanning the area. The hole brought them out behind the neighboring tomb, giving even more cover and putting them an aisle away from the gunfight. In the distance she heard the sounds of sirens, which meant the authorities would be here soon.

Getting shot was low on her priority list. Getting arrested for tomb-robbing didn't rank much higher.

"Move it," she hissed at Rick.

He pushed the relic through first. Then his backpack. She snatched them both up and leaned against the neighboring mausoleum, staying out of the thin gap between crypts where stray bullets might find them. Or one of the people shooting might notice them sneaking out.

Just as Rick had his upper body through the hole, a loud voice rang out over the shooting and the gunfire stopped.

Rick froze. Amber froze and stared at him in horror.

Oh no. Now what?

TWENTY-TWO

THE SILENCE in the cemetery after all the shooting stopped made Amber's ears ring. She held her breath, staring at Rick where he hung halfway out of the hole in the crypt. The night breeze did nothing to cool her warm cheeks or the sweat coating her back as she slipped her backpack on again.

"Give us the relic," a man on the other side of the crypts said. "And we'll let you leave and get him to a hospital."

"Fuck you," someone said. Amber was pretty sure that was the man from the doorway.

"You can't win," the original speaker said. "There are more of us. And your boss is wounded. All Kalashnik wants is the relic."

"He only wants it because I do!" The Russian this time, his voice hoarse.

"Is there any other reason to want a thing?" the original speaker said.

Amber gave Rick as sour look. She could not believe they were in the middle of a crime-boss pissing match to see who owned the rarest artifact.

Except she was pretty sure Mikhailov didn't want Galileo's pulse rate machine just for show and bragging rights. And if what Rick said was true, about Kalashnik assassinating Mikhailov's sons, she had a pretty good idea what Mikhailov *did* want the relic for.

Kalashnik must be someone the Russian couldn't get away with murdering. Someone he couldn't touch with the more conventional revenge methods. But his revenge plan would fall through if Kalashnik stole the relic right out from under him. Maybe. Unless Kalashnik didn't know what the relic could really do?

Questions she had no intention of asking either man. Her intention was to get the hell out of there.

She motioned Rick to hurry. He scrambled the rest of the way out of the crypt, pushing against the rocky rubble just outside the narrow hole left by the missing stone. He ducked behind the neighboring tomb with her, his back to the crypt as they held still and silent. Listening to the men shout back and forth at each other.

"Mikhailov is injured," Rick said near her ear.

She nodded. She'd heard the strain in his voice, too.

"That's going to make him very dangerous."

"Thought he was that already."

"Fair point."

She looked around and saw the same cat from inside the tomb—at least she thought it was the same cat—swishing its tail from on top of a mausoleum across from them. Its yellow eyes bright in the ambient city light as it licked its paws, unconcerned with the human fight.

"How do we get out of here now?" she asked.

The cat jumped off the mausoleum and jogged down the stone path in a direction opposite the one they'd used to find the tomb.

Rick glanced at the cat, then over his shoulder at all the

shouting men.

"Follow the cat," he whispered.

"The cat's going the wrong way," she said.

"There's a worker's entrance on this side of the cemetery somewhere. Plus, that cat's moving away from the fight."

Even as he said that, the gunfire started again.

She ducked and winced at the same time. "Follow the cat?"

"Follow the cat," Rick said.

They both stood and ran after the cat, ducking and keeping behind the cover of as many of the tombs as they could.

Shouts and cursing and gunfire behind them. Some screams.

Rick stayed at her back as she raced after the black and white cat. It dipped between two tombs that were too close together to allow her and Rick to pass.

"Follow the cat," she muttered. "How exactly?"

"Go around. Get to the back wall. We can follow the wall to the exit."

She hurried through the pathways until they'd reached the red brick wall. "Which way?"

Rick nodded to the right.

Where the cat sat staring at them.

Next to a small metal door.

"We're going to set off an alarm if we leave through here," she said.

"There's a gunfight going on behind us. You think anyone will notice?"

"Right." She gave the cat a nod of thanks.

It licked its front paw like it hadn't seen her.

She rolled her eyes, pushed the handle across the door, and almost fainted when it opened without them needing a key.

An alarm blared. Sirens closed in on the area.

Amber and Rick ducked into a nearby alley, waiting to see if anyone followed them out of the cemetery.

When no one did, not even one of the cats, Rick nodded, and

they made their way back to the Jeep, walking as leisurely as two tourists might on a night out in Buenos Aires.

While carrying a priceless relic.

TWENTY-THREE

INSPECTOR HAVIARD DROPPED into the plastic seat next to Amber as she and Rick waited to board their flight from Buenos Aires back to the U.S. by way of Italy. The departures lounge was crowded and noisy, the smell of too many people in one place filtered through excellent air conditioning that nevertheless did nothing for the sweat that broke out along Amber's back. She tightened her hold on the large bag in her lap and gave the inspector a bland look.

"Fancy seeing you here," Inspector Haviard said, giving Amber a tight smile.

"Strange, right? What are the odds?"

"What brings you all the way to Argentina, Inspector?" Rick asked, using his best I'm-innocent-there's-nothing-to-see-here smile.

"I was following a…lead. Did you hear about the trouble at Recoleta?"

"There was something on the news," Amber said, nodding to the television screens hanging over the seating area.

"Didn't catch most of it," Rick said. "My Spanish isn't that good. What did it say?"

Haviard raised her brows at Rick's pretty obvious lie. But she didn't comment on it. Instead, she said, "It looks like Jacque's murderer has been killed."

"Really?" Amber widened her eyes. "So you were able to find out the identity of said murderer."

Haviard nodded. "He and several of his men, some of the ones who've been with him for a long time, were all killed in a shootout with a rival gang."

"Wow," Amber said.

"That's just awful," Rick added.

"It was a mess," Haviard said. Not commenting on the awfulness or not awfulness of the many dead criminals. "But it closes the case on Jacque's murder. When I saw you, I thought that news might be of interest to you."

"Oh, it is," Rick said.

"Glad to know justice was served," Amber added.

"Justice." Haviard sucked in a deep breath as she scanned the busy airport, the throngs of people rushing past, tugging their carry-ons, hurrying to their flights, the noise and shouts of multiple languages filling the large terminal. She nodded a little, her gaze distant. Then she glanced back at Amber and Rick. "Sure. Justice."

Amber met her gaze without blinking.

"There's some talk that something might have been stolen from one of the tombs in the cemetery near the fight," Haviard said. "I don't suppose you'd know anything about that?" She studied both Rick and Amber as she asked, her expression direct but unreadable.

"Haven't heard anything about stolen tomb relics," Rick said. "Any idea what might have gone missing? Maybe we can keep our ear out for information. In my line of business…you hear things."

"I'm sure you do," Haviard said. "We don't know what went

missing. None of the men taken alive after the firefight are talking."

"Shame," Amber said.

"Yeah, real shame," Rick repeated.

"But if we do learn the truth," Haviard said, "I'll be sure to be in touch."

"You do that," Rick said.

"We'd be happy to help," Amber added with as much insincerity as was possible to convey in the short sentence.

Haviard raised her brows. "Have a safe flight." She rose, her gaze back to skimming the crowd. "Careful who you deal with next time. Maybe stick to restorations instead of forgeries."

She walked away before Amber or Rick could comment.

"I'm not sure whether to like her or hate her," Amber said.

"Caution and wariness are the appropriate responses. Caution and wariness."

"She wears really great shoes, though." This pair had been a low heel. black strappy sandal with a few black stone embellishments.

"Yes, she does," Rick agreed with a nod.

"She doesn't know about Galileo's pulse rate machine."

"If she does, she's not saying so out loud."

"If she does, she's letting us take it out of Argentina," Amber whispered near Rick's ear.

"And probably going to have us followed so she knows what we do with it."

"Will she cause trouble for us?"

"Not after we return it to the museum."

"And in the future?"

Rick didn't answer.

But for the moment, they didn't need that answer. So long as Haviard wasn't going to arrest them now, the future could look after itself.

"She said Mikhailov is dead," Amber murmured. "You believe her?"

"We'll know soon enough."

"If he is, does that mean…we're safe? What about Kalashnik's people?"

"Hopefully the mess here keeps everyone occupied long enough to forget all about us. If Kalashnik ever knew what he was really after, what he was trying to steal from Mikhailov, he'll learn soon enough it was never found."

Amber patted the larger backpack on her lap. New luggage to replace her old backpack. A sturdy piece she'd purchased at a luggage store as far from the Recoleta as it was possible to get.

"Probably best it was never found," she said.

"Definitely for the best," Rick said.

TWENTY-FOUR

One week later

AMBER LOOKED up from the clock on her workbench when someone cleared their throats. Rick O'Neill filled the doorway of her restoration workroom, looking ridiculously handsome and smug.

"Love the headpiece," he said. "Really brings out your eyes."

She snorted and set her magnifier headset aside. "How's Giuseppe doing?"

"Good. Delighted, grateful, relieved. All the expected emotions."

"Will he put it on display?"

After returning the relic to the Museo Galileo, putting it directly into Giuseppe's hands, and then confirming Diona was well and repairs to her workshop were underway, Amber had hurried back to New York in the hopes of keeping her job at the Met. They were all pretty sure Kalashnik wouldn't come after them, especially now that Mikhailov was dead. So she'd felt secure in returning. But she'd left before Giuseppe had decided what to do with the pulse rate machine.

"It's going into the vault for now," Rick said. "Given what it's supposedly able to do... He finally decided a little research might be in order first."

"Do you really think it can do what Essa thought it did?" She lowered her voice. "Do you think it can stop hearts?"

"I think...it's probably best if that remains a secret."

A part of her desperately wanted to know the truth. But a larger part of her thought, given there were people like Mikhailov in the world, Rick was right. There were some things better left unknown.

He moved into the room, leaning against her wooden workbench and looking at the fifteenth century clock she was restoring, some of the little metal gears still scattered on the table as she cleaned years of age and grime off them. "Giuseppe was very grateful to have the letters and notes his mother had hidden inside the bottom of the box. But I think that was for more personal reasons than professional."

"Can't blame him. Kind of agree with him about displaying the relic, too. Probably for the best if people continue to think it's just a myth."

Rick nodded. "Glad you got your job back."

"Well, when the Director of Special Collections at the Museo Galileo calls your boss to sing your praises for the excellent and last-minute restoration you did on a priceless piece of science history, your boss tends to forgive the little things. Like disappearing suddenly. And stealing his keys."

"What keys?"

"Nothing." She waved that away. "Thanks for getting Giuseppe to make that call. I'd have missed this job."

"I know." He grinned. "Guess this means you won't murder me now?"

"Well, you did keep me from getting killed. That has to count for something."

The news of what went down in the Recoleta Cemetery had

spread fast through the underground whisper network. Mikhailov had been confirmed killed in the firefight. Most of the people involved in the gunfight had either died or been arrested. No one was talking.

In the end, everyone assumed it had been some sort of plot for Mikhailov to assassinate Kalashnik, but the plan went wrong for Mikhailov.

Amber was a little amazed at how close those rumors got to the truth.

More rumors flew that Mikhailov's men were being killed, too. One by one. A kind of cleanup. Those same rumors claimed it was Kalashnik doing the cleanup. Amber was just glad to be out of the middle of the mess. None of the rumors hinted that Kalashnik was coming after her or Rick. She'd take that news.

"So are you here just to ensure I'm not going to murder you?" she asked Rick, leaning back in her seat and crossing her arms.

"That. And I have a peace offering."

"Peace offering? For what?"

"For getting you mixed up in this mess. With the Russian. With the relic."

"Are you kidding? I wouldn't have missed the chance to see that in real artifact for all the world. How many times in one lifetime do you get to see a mythical, lost relic in person?"

"While lots of people are shooting at you?"

"Okay. That part was bad. I'll accept a peace offering for that part."

"Good. Take a break. Grab your purse." He stood away from the table.

She narrowed her eyes at him. "Where are we going?"

He grinned. That ridiculously charming grin that made her both want to roll her eyes and left her feeling a little silly and giddy inside.

"What are you up to?" she asked as she stood and got her purse.

"Trust me."

"No. Where are we going?"

He chuckled. "I'm taking you shoe shopping."

Her turn to grin. "I knew you secretly loved me."

"So you're definitely not going to murder me now?"

"My murder plans have been suspended."

"Because I'm buying you shoes?"

"Because you're buying me shoes."

"Perfect." He put a hand to her lower back as he guided her out of the workroom. "Just remember this the next time I get you mixed up in another mess."

TWENTY-FIVE

Two weeks later

VICTOR WAS SHOWN into the large, dark office in the unmarked building a few blocks from the Kremlin. Kalashnik sat behind an ostentatious oak desk, his hands steepled in front of him. He was a small, skinny man, with glasses hanging off his hooked nose. His dark eyes were too large for his face. His brown hair unnaturally thick for a man his age. Dressed in an expensive suit and tie. Projecting the exact image he intended.

He motioned to a seat across from the desk. "I was sorry to hear about your boss, Victor. You have my condolences."

"Thank you," Victor said. He didn't take the offered seat.

"What brings you here today?"

"With the…passing of my boss, it's become my responsibility to see to his men."

"Ah. Yes. Of course. Ever the loyal soldier."

"Many of those men are being quietly…retired. I'm here to request a stop to that."

"What makes you think I would have anything to do with something like that?"

"You're a man of great power. And if you were to make certain requests known generally, there are very few who would not follow those…requests."

Kalashnik leaned back in his chair, and considered Victor. Victor stood without flinching.

"I can see why Mikhailov kept you with him all these years," Kalashnik murmured. Then, "But why would I want to make this request? It is none of my business."

Victor lifted the wooden box he carried. The leather straps, tacked across the top of the aged wood, the lid closed with an elaborate, aged brass clip. "This was one of the last prizes my boss sought, before his untimely death. It's priceless. There's not another one like it in the world. Most don't even think it exists."

"Really?" Kalashnik's eyes glittered in the dim office light. "I didn't realize he'd recovered the…prize. I was under the impression it had vanished. Been destroyed."

"Rumors are often untrue. Or spread for very specific reasons."

"Yes. There are reasons for everything." Kalashnik settled his hands on his chair's armrests.

"And given that this—" Victor lifted the box a little more, and Kalashnik's gaze dropped to it, "—is so unique, so irreplaceable, I hoped it would be enough to ensure some… leniency for my boss's men. With your new, elevated status within the government, I'm sure you only want a peaceful transition."

Kalashnik's brows jumped up, but his gaze never left the box. "So. That is the real one?" He licked his lips.

"It is. Mikhailov destroyed the forgery in his anger."

Kalashnik smiled. "Of course he did. He always had a temper. Even back in school."

Victor didn't comment. He stood still as Kalashnik continued to stare at the relic. He only had a very vague idea of what had started the rivalry between his former boss and Kalashnik all those years ago—something to do with their different ideas about attaining power, and how to wield that power. Now that Mikhailov was dead, Victor wasn't likely to get the full story. He didn't need it. He was used to secrets he carefully refused to know.

"It is…unique," Kalashnik said, his gaze never leaving the box Victor held. "I have a taste for unique."

"Yes. One of a kind. Nothing else like it in the whole world." Victor nodded to Kalashnik's desk. "May I?"

Kalashnik nodded.

Victor placed the box in front of him. Then stepped back a few feet. "Please, look inside."

Kalashnik gave him a look.

"Your people checked before I came in. There's nothing there that might harm you."

Victor knew Kalashnik was accustomed to assassination attempts. Especially with things like poison. And radiation. His rightful paranoia was why he was still alive. Why Mikhailov had never succeeded in killing him. His people had gone over the relic with any number of scanners and swabs, checking for anything that might cause harm. Just as they'd scanned Victor to ensure he had no weapons on him.

Still Kalashnik hesitated, his gaze narrowed on Victor.

"Would you feel more comfortable if I opened it for you?" Victor said. "A show of good-faith."

Kalashnik's smile managed to be both condescending and sly. "That would be good. Yes. Open it."

Victor approached the desk with his hands in plain sight, ensuring Kalashnik knew he wasn't carrying any weapons. Not that he'd have been allowed in here with weapons. Still, it was important to make it clear he was not armed in any way.

Holding Kalashnik's gaze, he opened the lid, lowering it back to reveal the contents of the box.

After a moment, when nothing happened, Kalashnik looked down. "Ah," he said with a sigh. "Exquisite."

He ran a finger over the cylindrical brass pendulum with its pointed tip, over the knotted piece of blue cloth that served as its chain. The folded ruler against one wall of the box. The plain iron disk with the astrological symbols on it.

"Do you know," Kalashnik said, "I have heard some rumors of what this device is capable of."

Victor kept his gaze on the wall opposite when Kalashnik looked up at him. He kept his expression neutral, showing no reaction to Kalashnik's comment.

"I've heard Galileo invented a way to stop hearts with this machine."

Victor continued to stare at the wall without responding.

"Should we try it out, Victor? See if that's true?"

"I wouldn't recommend it," Victor said.

From the corner of his eyes, he saw Kalashnik smiled. "Wouldn't you? Afraid I'll stop my heart?"

"No."

"Afraid I'll kill you with it?"

"No."

"Why not? I would like to see if it really works."

Victor finally looked down, meeting Kalashnik's gaze. "You want to know if it can stop hearts?"

"Oh yes. I would like to know that. Very much."

Victor snatched up the pendulum and plunged the pointed tip into Kalashnik's neck, piercing the artery three times in rapid succession.

Kalashnik's eyes widened comically behind his glasses. He grabbed at his throat, attempting to stop the rapid pumping of blood flowing out over his neck and down his perfectly tailored suit. He gurgled something, slammed a hand at his desk.

Victor pushed the chair away, rolling it backward across the polished marble floor, so Kalashnik couldn't trigger any alarms.

Then he stood patiently watching Kalashnik bleed. He dropped the pendulum back into the box and folded his hands together in front of him as he waited.

Kalashnik dropped from his seat, attempted to crawl across the floor. Blood pooled around him, squirting out with ever thump of his heart.

As his movements slowed, as he dropped to the elegant Turkish rug that carpeted a section of the cold black marble floor, Victor said, "It seems it does work. It stops hearts. Just as rumored."

He moved around to squat down in front of Kalashnik, staring him in the eyes as the man continued to make choking noises and the blood pooled thick under his body.

"That was for my boss. Payback for what you did to his sons."

When Victor rose, Kalashnik's gaze followed him and he reached out weakly for Victor. But his hand fell to the carpet and the choking noises stopped. Along with Kalashnik's breathing.

Victor watched for several minutes longer, ensuring the man was dead. Ensuring he'd meted out the revenge his boss had wanted.

By the time Kalashnik's people realized something was wrong and came slamming into the office, it was too late.

Victor had already walked right out the door, disappearing into the cold spring night.

THANK YOU

Thank you for reading GALILEO'S PENDULUM! I hope you enjoyed the globe-trotting adventure with a science history twist. This won't be Ross and O'Neill's last adventure either.

When I wrote this book, I was really feeling some nostalgia for older action-adventure movies like *The Mummy* (1999—Brendan Fraser and Rachel Weisz version), *Romancing the Stone*, and *Indian Jones*—particularly *The Last Crusade*. And I couldn't help a little sneaky, but probably too subtle, *Ghostbusters 2* reference at the end. There's also a movie I'm pretty sure only a dozen people outside my immediate family have seen that I just love called *Hudson Hawk* that has a big influence on me here. It's a ridiculous movie with lots of impossible, implausible stuff happening, and is just so super fun and entertaining. So shout out to the other dozen people who love that movie with me! Like *Hudson Hawk*, I wanted to write something with a science history element, even if parts of the "history" are made up. I hope I've done my inspiration justice, and created a fun tale for readers.

Obviously, because this is fiction, I took a lot of literary license with the history (a *lot*!), but the story of Galileo supposedly inventing an accurate pulse rate measurement device after being inspired by the swing of a lamp on a long chain during a church service in Pisa is a real story written by his biographer, Vincenzo Viviani. The story became well known, but was eventually considered apocryphal by science historians for the very reasons mentioned in my book—the specific lamp referenced by Viviani wasn't installed in that particular church until well after Galileo had moved away from Pisa. And Galileo didn't argue over the priority of his supposed invention when the physician Santorio Santorio invented one of his own.

But I liked the story and wanted to play with the idea. Obviously, I embellished and made some things up. Lots of things were made up. That's the fun part of fiction.

One of the best books I read when researching this story was GALILEO AND THE SCIENCE DENIERS by Mario Livio. It's a really excellent book. If you have an interest in Galileo's life and complicated relationship with the Catholic church, I highly recommend picking this one up.

Thanks again for reading GALILEO'S PENDULUM! I hope you had fun.

~Kat

BOOKS BY KAT SIMONS

Ross and O'Neill Adventures

Galileo's Pendulum

Percy James Mysteries

Movies May Murder

Coming 2023

MORE BOOK BY KAT SIMONS

Paranormal Romance

Tiger Shifters Series

Romancing the Leopard: A Tiger Shifters-Cary Redmond Crossover Novel

Urban Fantasy

The Cary Redmond Series

Cary Redmond Short Stories

Demon Witch Series

Contemporary Fantasy

Haunts and Howls Collections

Joan of Kerry Series

Tombstone Wizard

The Unshattered Sword

Destiny Through the Cats Eyes

Going Out of Business: Everything's for Sale

Contemporary Romances

Designed for You

Poinsettias and Possibilities

Coming December 2022

ABOUT THE AUTHOR

Award-winning, bestselling author, Kat Simons' debut action-adventure thriller, GALILEO'S PENDULUM, brings a mix of science history and fast-paced adventure to a little light forgery as her heroes race around the world to save an ancient relic. Her upcoming action-adventure mystery stories combine similar elements of adventure, world travel, and science—some of Kat's favorite topics.

She's also writing a soft-boiled, amateur sleuth series set in New York City. Not known for being a popular cozy mystery location, Kat wanted to show that even big cities can have small neighborhoods with a close-knit feel. From that idea, she started her Percy James series about the adventures and exploits of a front desk receptionist working in a boutique hotel on the Upper East Side of Manhattan. Percy James sees a lot in that small hotel. And not all of it is legal. The first stories in this new series debut in 2023.

After traveling the world, living in places like Hawaii, Germany, and Ireland, where she got her Ph.D. in animal behavior, Kat now lives in New York City with her family and a library's worth of books.

**For more on Kat and her future books,
you can find her at**

Website: https://www.katsimons.com
Newsletter: https://bit.ly/KatSimonsNewsletter
Facebook Page: https://www.facebook.com/KatSimonsAuthor
BookBub: https://www.bookbub.com/authors/kat-simons
Instagram: https://www.instagram.com/isabokelly/
Twitter: https://twitter.com/IsaboKelly